AF102974

Cinder's Trial

Fairytale Bureau
Book Two

Eve Langlais

Cinder's Trial © 2023 Eve Langlais

Cover by Addictive Covers © 2023

Produced in Canada

Published by Eve Langlais

http://www.EveLanglais.com

E-ISBN: 978 177 384 4961

Print ISBN: 978 177 384 4978

ALL RIGHTS RESERVED

This book is a work of fiction and the characters, events and dialogue found within the story are of the author's imagination and are not to be construed as real. Any resemblance to actual events or persons, either living or deceased, is completely coincidental.

No part of this book may be reproduced or shared in any form or by any means, electronic or mechanical, including but not limited to digital copying, AI training, file sharing, audio recording, email and printing without permission in writing from the author.

Prologue

Many years before the events in Hood's Caper...

The invitation for the masquerade ball took me by surprise. I'd not expected anything when I filled out the form for the contest being run by our local rock station, but the golden ticket, hand-delivered to me at work, indicated I'd won.

What would I wear? I couldn't exactly afford anything chic on my minimum wage salary. My tiny attic apartment cost me most of my paycheck. A good thing my work let me eat leftovers for free or I'd be starving.

Luckily, I enjoyed thrifting. The vintage store a few blocks from my place had a lovely gown in a light rose hue marked down due to a tear and a stain. With a little help from the attic spiders, who were wizzes with thread, and the mice who'd taken up residence under my bed, we turned the shabby gown into something presentable.

Dare I say I even looked like a princess? So long as no one glanced under the hem to see my battered ballerina flats.

Since I couldn't get the day off work—and I still needed to pay rent—I brought my dress with me and hung it in the employee break room. It led to questions and criticism from my coworkers.

"How did you get an invite?"
"I can't believe they're going to let you in.'"
"It's probably because she slept with someone."

I ignored them all. I'd spent a good portion of my childhood listening to the taunts of my stepmom and stepsisters. I lived by the mantra that being pushed in front of cars and shoved down stairs would break my bones but words couldn't hurt me.

You know what did hurt? The jealousy someone exhibited at the end of my shift, which turned out to be a half-hour longer than everyone else since I got assigned kitchen cleanup when we closed at nine, an hour after the ball started. I didn't let it bother me because, after all, didn't everyone say it was good to be fashionably late?

I finished putting away all the dishes and scrubbed the stovetops before heading to the break room to change. At least I wouldn't have to wait for a taxi. The hotel with the massive ballroom would only be a ten-minute walk.

Only it turned out I wouldn't be going to the ball after all.

I stared in shock at my dress, ripped from the hanger and tossed to the floor, trampled and torn. The maliciousness shouldn't have stunned me, and yet I found myself silently sobbing, fat tears rolling down my cheeks.

So much for having something nice for once.

As I lifted the rag from the floor and balled it up for the garbage, the air suddenly felt strange. Charged even, kind of like that weird sensation you got before a storm.

Poof.

I blinked my eyes, and yet the woman with gray hair in the bouffant dress remained floating a few inches above the floor.

"Hello, Cinderella. I am your fairy godmother, here to ensure you go to the ball," a claim punctuated by the twirl of a wand, which emitted light sparks.

My mouth rounded. "A what?" Given my mom insisted on naming me Cinderella, I'd read the story that pertained to my name. However, I didn't recall ever hearing about any fairy godmothers. In the original Grimm books, the woodland creatures helped

Cinderella. "The original Grimm Story of The Little Ash Girl didn't have a fairy godmother," I objected. "In that tale, the tree planted by the heroine's mother's grave was the one granting wishes." A tree I didn't have since my mom was buried in a graveyard that only allowed grass.

"Because your curse is one of the few that includes some aspects from modern adaptations," Godmother softly chided. "Now, just accept that I'm your fairy godmother, here to make your wishes come true."

"How?"

"Magic, of course. Now we don't have much time. Put on your dress."

"But it's ruined." I pointed out the obvious.

"Not for long. Hip, hop. The clock is ticking."

Despite living in a world where fairytales could come true, I remained skeptical as I put on the rag I'd worked so hard on.

"Shoes, too," she insisted.

I slid the scuffed slippers onto my feet.

"Excellent! Now hold still while I do my thing." The Godmother waved her wand and sang, the words not any I understood but the effect proved astonishing. My ruined gown transformed, pink and poufy but also shimmering with gold to match the shoes on my feet.

The magic also coiled my hair into ringlets atop my head, and a glance in the mirror showed a light layer of makeup to accent my eyes and lips. The crowning touch, the intricate gold mask that covered half my face.

"Oh my," I exclaimed, stunned by the transformation.

"Perfect," declared Godmother. "Now you just need to get to the ball so you can enchant your prince."

Her use of "enchant" bothered. I'd seen pictures of the prince hosting, and he was old. So very old. I had no interest in catching his eye. I just wanted to dance and see all the beautiful gowns and tuxedos.

"Thank you so much," I gushed.

"You're welcome, dear girl. Off you go." Before I could say another word, Godmother waved her wand, and poof, I found myself standing on the sidewalk outside the grand hotel.

My entrance didn't go unnoticed. People murmured, and even the musicians playing paused, most likely because an old man with much gold braid and medals tottered for me.

"Ah, at last, a beauty worthy of a prince." Prince Henrick leered at me with his yellowed and gray teeth, the wrinkles on his face too numerous to count.

I could think of no polite way to refuse his demand we dance.

So I danced with the prince. Over and over. He seemed undaunted by the fact I kept moving his hands from my buttocks. Made no attempt to hide the fact he stared at my cleavage.

The evening I'd so looked forward to turned out to be not as wonderful as expected. Knowing the story, or should I say curse, I wasn't surprised the prince proposed to me as the hour approached midnight.

"You flatter me, Your Highness," I stated, tugging my hand from his clammy grip.

"We will marry, and you will bear little princes," he cackled.

Inwardly I shivered with revulsion, and when he leaned in to try and kiss me, I turned and fled. I ran out of the hotel and onto the sidewalk, clutching my bouffant skirt. As I fled, my heel got caught in a grate, but hearing shouts behind me, I left the shoe behind.

Once I kicked off the remaining transformed slipper, I put some distance between me and those pursuing. I sprinted all the way home and thought myself safe.

Only the prince wouldn't accept my rejection.

A search began for the mysterious woman he'd fallen in love with.

Me.

He put out a call to all the ladies who'd attended to present themselves, stating that whoever fit into the shoe I'd left behind would become his bride.

I didn't make an appearance at the public spectacle

that had dozens of women, many who'd never even gone to the ball, trying on the golden shoe. To my relief, someone managed to wedge her foot into that golden slipper—"someone" being Marilyn, a coworker who'd never been nice to me and deserved the gropy old prince as far as I was concerned.

That should have been the end of it, only my fairy godmother had the nerve to visit me a few days later wearing a frown.

"Cinderella, what's this I hear about you rejecting the prince?"

I arched a brow. "Can you blame me? He's old enough to be my great-grandfather."

My observation pursed Godmother's lips. "The Grimm Effect doesn't take age into account when pairing people."

"Well, it should, or maybe it should let people fall in love on their own," I huffed.

"Be that as it may, you appear safe from Prince Henrick. However, I'm afraid something must still be done with you."

I frowned. "Meaning what?"

"My failure to give you a happily ever has agitated the curse, and it's pressuring me to do something about you."

My eyes widened. "Wait, are you here to kill me?"

Godmother's eyes widened. "Goodness, no, dear

girl. However, you and I won't be done until I make your heart sing. Alas, I'm not aware of any eligible princes. Henrick was the only current, unmarried one. There is presently a worldwide shortage of eligible royalty."

"I'd rather not be forced into marriage to a stranger." I spoke the truth.

"Perhaps we can circumvent that aspect of your curse. After all, more than one thing can make you happy. Any suggestions, dear girl?"

I hesitated before saying, "I would have liked to expand my education after high school. I just can't afford it."

The suggestion pursed Godmother's lips. "Generating money is the one thing I can't do. Make carriages from pumpkins and other melons, yes. Transform rags into dresses, also doable, but cash..." She shook her head.

My shoulders slumped. I should have known better than to get my hopes up. Since when did good things happen to me? Look at how the ball turned out.

A snap of fingers drew my gaze to Godmother, who beamed. "I think I have just the thing for you. Tell me, have you heard about the new Fairytale Bureau?"

While it had been established only a few years before, I did know of it. They were supposed to help people caught up in the Grimm Effect.

"I'm familiar with them. Why?"

"What if I could get you into their academy?"

"I can't afford it." Like any other college, the tuition didn't come cheap.

"It wouldn't cost you a thing, and if you pass, it's a guaranteed job that will pay much better than what you're doing now."

An education and a career? "In that case, yes, please."

And so with a little magical help, I became a Fairy-tale agent, foiled the curse that wanted to marry me to a prince, and, years later, finally met the man who made my heart pitter-patter.

What a shame I also disliked him.

1

I sang as I worked in my kitchen, prepping some veggies for the salads I'd take in my lunches. Chicken grilled in a pan with butter and garlic gave me some protein, and fruit I'd already cubed and put into containers, a sweet finish. My little helpers scurried about giving me a paw, the troupe of mice—who'd been my constant companions since my teens—chirping in harmony with my song.

Some might question my allowing rodents to touch my food. To them I said nothing. I wasn't the confrontational type. Let them have their opinion. My mice were family and no dirtier than anyone else. Possibly even cleaner than some people I'd met in my life.

A peek at the window showed more of my friends, the robins, hoping for some treats. I threw up the sash, the screen in it long gone, and dumped a handful of seed in front of them and got some happy chirps in reply.

Those familiar with the Cinderella curse would understand my affinity for animals and the fact they were drawn to me. Always had been, even before my unfortunate encounter with the prince. When I jilted the old royal, I'd worried I'd lose my woodland friends. However, despite beating my curse, my gift and friends remained.

Once I finished my meals for the week and stowed them in the fridge, I pulled out some cheese, already cut into chunks, and the mice cheered—which for the curious emerged as a higher-pitched chirp.

As I fed them and thanked them by name—Rosy, Dora, Lester, Orville, Petunia, and Fred—the air got a strange electric feeling.

Then poof!

A woman of mature years, her silver hair bound in a bun, her face aged and yet smooth, appeared in my kitchen, wearing a billowy gown and holding a wand.

My fairy godmother, whom I'd not seen since I beat my curse.

"Oh no, not you again." Not exactly polite, but I couldn't stop the complaint from slipping out.

"It has been a while," Godmother agreed.

"Not long enough," I muttered. I'd matured since

then from a young girl of eighteen to one in her thirties.

My expression must have shown my displeasure, because Godmother huffed, "Most people would be happy to have a fairy godmother whose task is to make your wishes come true."

At her claim, I frowned and shook my head. "I already got my wish. I graduated from the Fairytale Academy with honors and have a great job with the bureau."

"But you're still single."

"I'm aware, but that doesn't mean I want or need a prince." Give me a normal man, one not bound to me by a curse.

To my surprise, Godmother smiled. "In that case, I've come to the right place."

"Excuse me?" I blinked at her odd reply.

"I want someone who is willing to reject the prince."

"I'm confused."

"I realize this might sound strange, but I'm here to help you escape your curse, permanently. But it won't be easy. The Grimm Effect has been more virulent of late."

"I'm aware." The escalation began a few months ago and I'd been one of the first to notice at the bureau—AKA the Fairytale Bureau, in charge of minimizing difficulties that arose as the Grimm Effect forced people to follow its stories. Many of those who'd managed to evade their Grimm curse had been finding themselves entangled in a new version, one darker than before—darker being kinder than saying bloody. A desperate edge had begun appearing as people, in the throes of magical compulsion, went to greater, more violent extremes to satisfy the terms of their curse.

Take my friend and colleague, Blanche Hood. She'd been embroiled in a serial murder mystery that resulted in her having to kill the huntsman, and now she lived happily with the wolf.

"It would seem the Grimm Effect isn't done with you," Godmother announced.

I shook my head. "But I'm not interested in completing my story. Hence you're wasting your time. Surely there's some other Ash Girl who'd welcome your aid?"

"Not any like you. And trust me, I'm not happy about my role. Like many people in this world, I am bound by the Grimm Effect and forced to do its bidding." Godmother's lips turned down.

"Oh, I didn't realize."

Godmother nodded. "There was a time when I thought by complying with the stories, I could perhaps put an end to it. Alas, the magic powering the Grimm Effect has only gotten stronger. But there is good news.

Some of the tales have been eradicated and those caught in them freed."

"Eradicated how?" I asked with a frown.

"I'm not sure. At first, I thought it a fluke, that the magic petered out for those particular tales. However, it appears that some have managed to counter their misfortune to the point it cancels the story entirely. For example, we recently had a Red Cap who somehow managed to wipe out that storyline entirely."

"So it's true," I murmured. "I'd noticed that the current Red Cap cases had pretty much vanished but thought perhaps we'd just not been very good at detecting new ones."

"It and a few others are no longer of concern, but of more importance, it means the Grimm Effect can be beaten!" Godmother's eyes gleamed with excitement.

"Which is great, but you said you don't know how."

Her lips turned down. "I wish I had a simple answer. I can only assume that those involved in those particular cases did something so completely out of the norm that the magic couldn't handle it."

"I rejected the prince, but that didn't stop the Cinderella curse," I pointed out.

"Because that's obviously not the key to ceasing that particular tale."

"Any suggestions?" Because I really didn't want to

have to fend off princes the rest of my life, which technically should be easy as long as I didn't attend any balls.

"I don't have any ideas, yet, but given the magic sent me here to force you back into that particular storyline, I'm thinking we have a chance to figure it out."

I arched a brow. "We?"

"I'd like to help you."

"Help me how, exactly?"

"That's the problem. No idea. I'm afraid we'll have to wing it, dear girl. But maybe together we can find a way to beat your curse."

"I don't know what you think you can do. I'm not even sure why you're here. I haven't been invited to any balls, and I'm not aware of any visiting princes."

Knock. Knock.

I swiveled to eye my door, mostly because people rarely knocked. My apartment, a massive, converted attic in a triplex, had too many stairs for most to brave.

The mice chittered, and my pet iguana, Izzy, padded to the door and stuck his tongue under the bottom edge before making a noise. Those who didn't have my gift would have heard a hiss. Me, I understood I had a delivery person waiting outside. Odd since I'd not ordered anything.

"Are you going to answer?" Godmother asked.

A part of me didn't want to. I feared what lay on the other side. Unlike Belle, another friend and colleague, and Blanche, I lacked courage. I avoided conflict. Often said yes to things I didn't want to just to appear agreeable.

Hence why I opened the door to see a man in uniform, not the kind used by the postal service or even any of the package delivery companies. The man at my door wore navy blue trimmed in silver with black knee-high boots and crisp, white gloves.

"Miss Cinderella Jones?" he queried.

"Yes. Can I help you?"

He held out a large envelope of white, embossed in silver and sealed in dark blue wax.

My stomach plummeted.

"This is for you." He held it out, and I didn't grab it.

"What is it? Who's it from?" I asked instead.

"His Royal Highness, Prince Killian the First, is formally inviting you to his fortieth birthday ball."

"No thank you." I politely refused.

"I'm sorry, miss. I think you misunderstand. This invitation is an honor."

"No, I understand perfectly and am simply not interested. Have a nice day." I shut the door and leaned against it as if the courier would force his way in and make me take the invitation.

He didn't. Instead, he slid it under my door so it could mock me.

My fairy godmother remained in my kitchen, sitting on a stool, feeding cheese to the mice, who didn't care it came from a stranger.

"Aren't you going to open it?" she asked.

"No, because I'm not going."

"If you say so."

"I'm not," I insisted.

"You know the curse won't let you off that easily."

Maybe not, but it was worth a try.

2

Despite having the mice dispose of the invitation, it reappeared the following morning, sitting on my kitchen counter, mocking me.

Still no.

I didn't know who this Prince Killian was, but he'd have to settle for a different Cinderella. A thought that reminded me of what happened the last time I'd rejected a prince. Old Henrick and my bitchy ex-co-worker Marilyn married, but she didn't live happily ever after. From what I'd gleaned from the news reports, Henrick discovered her lie and murdered her by stabbing her with the heel of the shoe.

A horrifying thing to happen and I'd spent years riddled with guilt over it. It took Belle repeatedly telling me, *"Play stupid games, win a fatal prize,"* to help me overcome my sense of responsibility. It wasn't my fault Marilyn lied, thus leading to her demise. Still... I felt bad.

I plucked the invitation—while wearing gloves to avoid skin contact—and took it to my kitchen sink, where I shoved it down the garburator hole and flipped the switch, grinding it to a pulp. Then I left for work.

Upon entering the bureau, I greeted the very pregnant Luanne, who was due to birth her yet another son any day now. Poor woman. While actually in love with her husband, they were under The Twelve Brothers curse. Meaning, if Luanne had the prerequisite dozen boys, followed by a girl child, all her sons would die. The plan was to get her tubes tied before she reached that number. She insisted she'd stop at ten to be safe, but I had my doubts. Luanne loved having babies.

Personally, the idea of birthing that many children horrified. I wanted one, maybe two max, if I ever met the right person—which, as the years passed, got less and less likely. It wasn't that I was picky, but I attracted the wrong sort. Men who leered and thought me a pushover. Males who wanted to treat me as a fragile damsel, good for looking pretty and keeping house. None recognized that, despite my affable nature, I did have a strong sense of worth and was intelligent enough to know what I wanted.

I wanted love, true love, and respect. Apparently, too much to ask for.

Upon arriving at my desk, I noticed the invitation to the ball sitting atop my keyboard.

My lips pinched. Bloody magic trying to force me to its will.

Too bad. I still wasn't opening it. By lifting my keyboard, I dumped it into the waste bin beside my desk. With it out of the way, I went to work. The Grimm Effect had been in overtime of late, as we'd been seeing a surge in cases.

Pigs, swans, rats, and a bevy of creatures had been spotted in our city causing trouble. We had some Rumpelstiltskin wannabes making bargains for babies. Rapunzels looking for princes. Fiddlers fiddling and sly foxes scheming. We'd even had to ban apples since they kept putting people into magical comas.

In the early years, it used to be that only the original Grimm stories and some adaptations were re-enacted. But no one could deny anymore that the repertoire of curses had expanded to include more stories.

So many stories that at times I wondered why we even bothered.

My gaze went to the corner of the envelope peeking from my trash bin. Given most of the field agents were currently handling cases, and I had no new data to work with yet, I found myself doing a search on Prince Killian. Ruler of Corsica, a small European island that separated from France in the early 1900s, he was the only heir to his mother's throne.

To my surprise, the image on file showed he wasn't hideous. On the contrary, his golden hair went nicely with his olive skin tone and brilliant green eyes. A fit prince, he played polo, swam, jogged. Or at least the paparazzi had posted pics of him doing those various physical activities. They also had him in uniform, inspecting his army.

Someone snuck up on me to remark, "Oh good, you're already studying Prince Killian."

Surprise had me whipping around in my seat to exclaim, "I wasn't studying him."

"You should be since he's your next assignment," Hilda, my boss, stated in that no-nonsense tone she liked to use with her staff.

"Excuse me?"

"Prince Killian is arriving today and will be conducting some meetings with government officials to hammer out some treaties between our countries. As well, he will be the guest of honor at a ball being thrown for his fortieth birthday at the Classica Hotel. To ensure his protection while on U.S. soil, we've deployed the Grimm Knights."

"Alright." I nodded. The Grimm Knights were Grimphers—people caught by the Grimm curse—who'd been turned into heroes and now thrived on saving the world while working for the bureau. "Do you need me to do some reconnaissance?"

"No. I'm assigning you to act as the liaison between the prince and the bureau."

"You can't be serious," I huffed. "He's a bachelor royal."

"I'm aware."

"Are you aware I've gotten a very insistent invitation to his ball?" I pointed to the garbage can, where the edge of the envelope peeked.

"Well, of course you are invited. How else would you be able to assist him?"

"Assist him doing what?" I squeaked.

"Making sure none of the attending Cinderellas snares him in a trap," Hilda explained with a slight roll of her eyes.

"Wait, he doesn't want to get married?" That would be a first. Most princes loved the adulation and attention of prospective brides.

Hilda smiled. "Like a certain employee of mine, he's determined to escape the curse. However, that won't be easy. For one, the ball was his mother's idea. Apparently, she wants some heirs."

"Wait, she wants him to follow the story?" How appalling. You'd think his own mother would want him to choose the woman he'd spend his life with.

"Oh yes, Queen Melania is quite determined to see

him wed. And she might get her wish. According to the most recent reports, the number of Cinderellas suddenly showing up in our city has been increasing daily. The curse is transforming them left and right. The office that handles legal name changes can't keep up."

I blinked. "Exactly how many Cinderellas are we talking about?"

"At last count, the curse has invited one hundred and thirty-six."

My jaw dropped. "That many? That's insane. There aren't even that many bachelor princes in the world." Princes didn't stay single for long these days, given they were in short supply.

"Hence why the prince requested aid."

I rubbed my forehead. "Exactly how do you expect me to somehow keep more than a hundred hopeful ladies from trying to trap him?"

"Not easily, which is why the Grimm Knights will be assisting."

"And will they be killing the Cinderellas that get too frisky?" The Knights had a reputation, especially their oversized, dour leader, Levi.

"Their orders are to detain and-or remove problematic hopefuls."

I waved a hand. "Why is the ball being held here?

Shouldn't this prince be celebrating his birthday at home?"

"Unfortunately, given the time-sensitive nature of some of the goods the treaties will be covering, it had to be now. And, as mentioned, his mother saw an opportunity she didn't want to miss."

"Fine. However, can't someone else act as liaison? You know the curse has been reactivating toward people who'd already evaded it, and apparently, I might be next." I pointed to the trash bin. "I've gotten rid of that invite several times already, but it keeps popping back up."

Hilda glanced briefly at the bin before looking back at me with a regretful expression. "About the whole reactivation thing, there've been a few video meetings with the higher-ups in the bureau about that matter. The consensus by some of the scientists studying it is that those experiencing a resurgence didn't actually beat their curse so much as cause it to go dormant until the right situation presented itself."

"Doesn't that make it even more risky to use me as his liaison? I don't want to have to reject him like I did Prince Henrick." Who ended up in front of a firing squad because, despite being a prince, murdering one's wife and throwing her corpse from a parapet remained illegal.

"You needn't worry about Prince Killian. Like you,

he's very determined to not succumb to the Grimm Effect trap."

My lips pursed. "Thought by many a person who fell victim. I really would prefer it if you sent Belle or Blanche. Even better, what about Rory and Tom?" As straight men, they wouldn't be tempted by the male prince.

"Rory and Tom are dealing with a family of bears squatting in the west end. Blanche is a touch too abrasive for someone this important. As for Belle, she met the prince when he got off the plane, and let's just say, it didn't go well." Hilda's lips pursed.

"What did she do?"

"Mistook him for a thief when he grabbed his suitcase from the luggage carousel. She tackled him to the ground."

"She arrested the prince?" I couldn't help an incredulous note.

"In her defense, he didn't look very royal in his jeans and rockband T-shirt."

I almost grinned at the thought of the prince being taken down by Belle. "I'm surprised she got close enough, given he's being protected by the Knights."

"The Knights didn't expect a threat from Belle. Luckily, the incident amused the prince. However, I still thought it best to reassign her."

I sighed. "I've got a bad feeling about this." Then,

because maybe it would help, I murmured, "My fairy godmother visited me last night."

Hilda's eyes widened. "Uh-oh."

"Exactly. So you can see why I might be leery about accepting this task."

"Or you could look at this as a chance to put your story to bed for another decade or two."

My boss wouldn't be swayed, and as she left me to stare at my screen, I wondered what I could do to ensure this prince never looked at me twice.

Maybe if I didn't shower and showed up sweaty? A little too gross.

I could dress in ugly, shapeless clothes and find something atrocious to wear for the ball. I would make sure I didn't wear slippers but tightly laced boots. I'd refuse to dance with him. I'd use my words and say no.

"Excuse me, are you Agent Jones?" a deep voice asked.

I said, "Yes," before I turned around to see the very pretty prince standing by my desk.

3

Prince Killian looked even more handsome in person than in his online images and, as I'd been warned by my boss, didn't appear royal given he wore jeans with holes in the knees and a T-shirt emblazoned with Jim Morrison's head.

"Hi, I'm Killian." He held out his hand to shake.

I eyed it and shook my head. "Sorry, but I make it a point to avoid touching royalty."

Rather than be offended, Killian grinned. "I'd avoid it if I could too, but it might make it hard to pee."

My mouth rounded in surprise before I giggled. "I'm pretty sure you're breaking all kinds of protocol saying that."

"I know I am. My mother reminds me at every turn how unprincely I am. In my defense, I spent most of my life growing up as an ordinary chap. Mum kept me away from palace politics for the first half of my life."

"That's unusual."

He shrugged. "I'm thankful she did. Sometimes I kind of wish I still lived in the country."

"Your Highness!" The title was barked by Levi, who stalked toward us with a glower. His salt and pepper hair had been recently cut short and emphasized the sharp angles of his cheeks and fresh-shaven jaw.

"Uh-oh, you're in trouble," I whispered.

Killian's smile widened. "I guess me telling my babysitters I didn't require them to be glued to my ass didn't work."

"You know they're only doing their job."

A reminder that had Killian grimacing. "A waste of resources if you ask me."

The imposing Knight halted a pace from the prince and glowered. "What did I say about waiting for one of us to go ahead and ensure your safety?"

The prince rolled his shoulders. "I'm in the Fairytale Bureau. How much safer can it get?"

The answer didn't appease Levi, who crossed his bulky arms over an even thicker chest. "For a man who's determined to avoid marrying a Cinderella, you ran straight for the nearest one."

"Can you blame me?" Killian winked in my direction.

Levi's piercing gaze bored into me, and I resisted an urge to stick out my tongue. Levi took everything so seriously. Usually commendable, but he matched his rigidness with a brusque attitude. A good thing he rubbed me wrong, as it helped me to not admire the width of his shoulders, shoulders only slightly wider than the prince's.

I waved a hand at Levi. "Your prince is safe around me. I have no intention of being dragged to the altar, curse or not." A hot declaration that I meant. Killian might be handsome and funny, but being married to royalty sounded awful. All those rules and people watching all the time... Ugh.

"As if the Grimm Effect cares what you want," Levi snapped back.

I arched a brow. "I beat it once. I'll beat it again. And you should know it's possible. After all, look around us." All bureau agents were Grimphers—curse survivors. People who'd told the Grimm Effect to take a hike because they weren't conforming.

My reply pinched Levi's lips. "You're testing my patience, Agent Jones."

"Can't handle someone not kowtowing to your demands?" my sharp riposte. Funny how only Levi brought out the sassy in me.

"I've been tasked with keeping the prince safe, and he's being uncooperative. So don't encourage his bad behavior." The glare swiveled to the prince, who didn't look the least bit chastised.

"I can't blame him for chafing at having shadows," I declared. "How would you like being followed twenty-four-seven?"

"I'd be appreciative and cooperative with those trying to keep me alive," Levi's stiff reply.

"For goodness sake. No one's trying to kill the prince," I huffed. "Your job is mostly to ensure overeager and conniving wannabe princesses don't compromise him while he's visiting."

"Hard to do if he keeps slipping those of us watching him."

"Foiled by a prince? That must sting." The taunt slipped out of me.

"You're not helping matters," growled Levi.

Killian's head bobbed back and forth between us before he said, "I take it the breakup went bad?"

"What?" we both exclaimed.

"It's obvious you two have a past," Killian stated with a shrug.

"Oh no we don't," I huffed. "As if I'd date *him*." I preferred my potential partners to be bookish and less kill-stuff-with-a-sword.

"I'm sorry, princess. Does my presence offend thee?" mocked Levi.

"Just your attitude. I shall eat popcorn and cheer the day someone adjusts it for you." Funny how I could be meek about certain things and around some people; however, something about Levi roused the prickly porcupine in me.

Killian sat his ass on the edge of my desk. "So, Agent Jones, I hear you're to be my liaison with the bureau. Not quite sure what that entails."

"Me neither," I admitted. "But given my specialty is digging for information and putting the pieces of it together, most likely, I'll be screening guests and ensuring Levi here doesn't accidentally decapitate someone you actually like."

"If they pose a threat, then I will do what I must," grumbled Levi.

"Without killing if you don't mind. We don't need a diplomatic incident," I reminded.

"I know how to do my job," Levi grumbled.

"Obviously, or you wouldn't be in charge of the Grimm Knights. I'm just suggesting you don't make a mess while doing it."

Killian spread his hands. "She is right. Blood is devilishly hard to rinse out of the uniforms my mother made me pack." He turned at me to confide, "They're white, which is very impractical, but she insisted."

My lips quirked. "I think we'll be seeing a lot of white from the hopefuls." A lot of Cinderella-cursed ladies tended to chase their princes in wedding gowns.

"I'm thinking we should discuss the ball and other things over lunch. Any suggestions?" Killian queried.

"Depends. Fancy sit-down, casual sit-down, or stand-up eating from something that can drive away?"

His laughter rang out. "Oh, Agent Jones. If I was in the market for a wife, you might just be perfect. Give me some diesel fumes with my meal, please."

"If you're feeling adventurous, I know a food truck that serves the most insane waffle sandwiches with fresh kettle chips."

"Lead the way, Agent Jones." Killian offered me a courtly bow, at odds with his appearance.

"My pleasure, Prince Killian." I rose from my desk and snared my purse.

"Let's avoid the prince part. Call me Killian. It will attract less attention in public that way."

"In that case, call me Cinder."

"I'm surprised you changed your name, given your stance on the curse," Killian remarked as we headed for the elevator, trailed by Levi, who continued to scowl.

"Actually, my mom named me Cinderella at birth because she loved that story growing up." Little did she know what would happen with the Grimm Effect.

"A pity the curse prefers the darker versions of the fairytales," Killian remarked as the elevator descended.

"Are the nicer ones really all that better, given the curse essentially removes free will?" Not entirely true but the manipulation by the Grimm Effect, which sometimes included transformation, often made it feel that way.

"You make a good po—aaah!"

The prince—and me, I might add—yelled as the elevator suddenly plunged!

4

WHEN THE ELEVATOR CRASHED AFTER letting go and plummeting, I didn't die. Mostly because a large male body cushioned me from impact.

The elevator hit the bottom of the shaft hard, rattling my teeth, eyeballs, and bones, and left me stunned atop someone. It took me a moment to blink my eyes into focus and find my face practically smooshed against Levi's.

I pulled back and managed a shaky, "That was unexpected."

His brow creased as he asked, "Are you okay?"

"Yes." I tried to push up from him but could only do so by touching his wide body and seating myself—AKA straddling his groin. I glanced over to see the prince braced in a corner, looking somewhat pale, and even better, I saw no blood.

"Are you injured?" I asked.

"Nope. Surprisingly fine. That was quite thrilling," the prince replied, straightening himself.

"I wonder what happened," I mused aloud. Elevators didn't suddenly fail without cause, and I knew we'd had ours recently serviced.

"Mind getting off me?" Levi grumbled. A reminder I still sat on him, and apparently a certain part of his body noticed.

The feel of his burgeoning erection under my backside had me scrambling to stand. "Sorry. I didn't mean to squash. Did I hurt you?"

"I'm fine. But I think we should get out of this coffin." Levi vaulted to his feet and slapped the open button. The doors, partially creased from impact, didn't budge.

"Try the emergency phone." I pointed to the red receiver.

The prince grabbed it and put it to his ear before shaking his head. "It's dead."

My lips pursed. "Most likely someone's noticed the elevator is out of commission. We just need to wait."

Levi sniffed. "Anyone smell smoke?"

I'd opened my mouth to say no when the odor hit me. "Something's burning."

An already grim Levi turned stonier. "We need to get out of here."

"Great idea, but how since the doors are stuck?" I pointed out the obvious.

"The hatch should still be accessible. We can climb out through there." Levi glanced overhead, and I saw the rectangular cutout in the ceiling of the cab.

"I'll go," Killian offered. "Give me a boost."

Levi shot it down. "You can't go first. If this was an attempt on your life, then there might be someone waiting in the shaft to finish you off. I'll go."

"If you go, then who protects the prince?" I pointed out.

"Protect him from what?" Levi glanced around with exaggeration.

"From whatever is trying to chew its way through the floor. Don't tell me you can't hear that?" I pointed to my feet.

The munching noise had taken me a moment to place before I realized it reminded me of my mice when we moved into the new place and they munched themselves new entrances in the walls for the homes they created.

"Fuck me," Levi muttered.

"You're not my type," Killian quipped, causing me to bite my lip because Levi's expression promised murder.

I poked the big Knight in the chest. "Stop glaring daggers at the prince and give me a boost."

"What?" He glanced down at me.

"You can't go, the prince can't go, but I can." I pointed upward. "Give me a boost, and I'll see if anything's waiting up there."

"It's too dangerous." Levi refused with a vigorous shake of his head.

"So is staying here." I then coughed, even though the smoke wasn't yet that bad. "And might I remind you that, as an agent, I am trained to handle danger." I didn't mention the fact that, while I had the training, I'd never really had to employ it, given I sat behind a desk.

"Take this." Levi pulled a dagger from a sheath and slapped it into my hand.

"I don't think so." I went to hand it back, but he scowled.

"You are not going up there without some kind of defense."

"Fine." I sighed and tucked it into my purse, which I slung cross-body. I'd left my suitcase by my desk, not wanting to lug it around for lunch. The suitcase contained items the bureau deemed necessary for its agents. Holy water, stakes, sleep potions, restraints, and, in my case, snacks in case I met new friends.

Levi knelt and cupped his hands. "If you see anything, you get back in here."

"Yes, sir," I chirped as I stepped into his waiting

palms. He lifted me with ease and high enough I had no difficulty shoving the hatch up and sideways.

Levi heaved me even higher so I barely had to do anything but flop onto the roof of the elevator, barely lit by the light coming up from the hole in the cab. The cable that should have held the elevator in place was gone, which explained why it fell. The smell of smoke appeared to be of the burning-oil variety. The mechanism that ran the elevator most likely hadn't shut off and strained.

"See anything?" Levi shouted.

"No. Hold on. Let me get the flashlight working on my phone." I beamed the cell upwards and saw an empty shaft. However, when I glanced over the edge of the elevator where the smoke rose from, I gasped at the number of glowing red pinpricks.

Levi heard. "What is it?"

"Rats," I whispered. "Lots of them." Now, you might wonder at my trepidation at seeing rodents. After all, I loved mice. Mice versus rats, though? Two different kinds of beasts. Mice tended to be docile and sweet. Rats were not. Not to mention most rats were infected by the Grimm Effect, making them do things out of character for their species. Say like decide to chew through the floor of an elevator. I'd bet they'd had something to do with the cable failure, too.

"I'm coming up," Levi stated.

"Wait. Let me see if I can talk to them."

By talk, I meant convince them to not attack. But how? I didn't have any food with me. Maybe I could use words and kindness to sway them.

"Hello." I offered a cheery greeting.

The pink-nosed rodent closest to me clung to the ladder bolted to the side of the shaft and twitched its whiskers.

"I don't suppose you'd let me and my companions pass?"

The rat bared its teeth and hissed before leaping to the roof of the cab to face off against me.

"I guess that's a no."

"What's happening?" Levi hollered.

"I think the rat wants to eat me." I went with honesty because it advanced on me with evil intent.

"Stand back, princess," Levi advised a second before he leaped to grab the edges of the hole. He hauled himself out just as the rat launched!

And got batted aside.

The big man made the space seem impossibly tight, but I wouldn't deny relief at him being there to handle the threat.

Levi snarled, "Okay, you mangy rodents. Let's get this over with."

The rat he'd batted aside had fallen between the

elevator and the shaft. Apparently, the others took note and fled.

The prince below us yelled, "The scratching stopped."

A relief of one sort, but the problem of the smoke remained.

Levi knelt down and put his hand in the hole. "Let's go, Your Highness, before the rats decide they are hungry after all."

Even I wasn't immune to admiration at the ease with which Levi hauled the not-so-tiny prince through the hatch.

"Now what?" I asked.

"We climb," Levi stated matter-of-factly.

I eyed the ladder and the distance to the next door, only faintly visible. Was now a good time to say I never managed a single pull-up during my bureau training? I wasn't out of shape, per se. However, I didn't exercise on a regular basis either, unless the stairs to my apartment counted.

Rather than orate my trepidation, I volunteered. "I'll go first. Killian, you take the middle, and Levi will cover our rear."

"And how exactly will you open the door, princess? Or are you packing more muscle than I can see?" Levi drawled, poking a hole in my plan.

"Good point," I conceded. "In that case, Levi, you go first, then the prince, then me."

Killian protested. "I don't like the idea of you being at the bottom if those rats return."

"I'll be fine." A lie, but an agent should be brave in the face of adversity—and they had a shot for rabies.

"Let's move quickly." Before he finished speaking, Levi began climbing, quickly reaching the next level, with Killian close behind. Since I didn't fancy having my face pressed against his heels, I waited on the roof of the elevator.

Levi grunted. "This one ain't budging. I'm going up to the next level."

He climbed the ladder upward, and Killian followed, but I got distracted by a noise. Make that noises. Scratching and clawing. The rats were coming back.

"Um, Levi, I think we have company."

"Climb!" he ordered from high enough overhead I couldn't see him.

I grabbed the first rung just as the first set of red eyes peeked over the cab. I'd climbed a few when the hissing had me glancing down to see the entire roof of the elevator covered in squirming bodies. Worse, they tried to climb the ladder after me. At least the smooth walls kept them from moving up them spider-like.

"I've got the door open," Levi shouted. "Move your asses."

Killian clambered quickly to safety, but I struggled, the rungs slippery in my sweaty grip. It didn't help that a rat suddenly latched onto my shoe.

I screamed and shook my foot until it flew off.

"What's going on, princess?" Levi hollered.

"What do you think?" I huffed. "Rats. Lots of them, and they can climb." They were also smart. I made the mistake of looking down to see them forming a rat pyramid, one that got higher as I watched. High enough one of them leaped for my leg.

I screeched. I know, not useful, and not something taught at the bureau's academy, but I didn't know what else to do but make noise as I swung my body sideways so it missed.

Something large fell past me and landed with a thump.

Levi had leaped from above and proceeded to kick the squirming rodents. They squealed as they scattered.

He barked, "Climb."

I faced the ladder and heaved myself up a rung. Then another. I squeaked as something nudged my foot, and I instinctively kicked.

"Whoa, princess. It's me. Stay still for a second."

I opened my mouth to ask why, only to lose my

voice as my breath rushed out. Levi shadowed my body, inserting his feet between mine, his body cocooning me from behind.

"I need you to face me and hold on tight," he stated.

"I can climb."

"Yeah, you can, but this will be faster."

I might have argued, but he had a point. With his arms caging me, I turned around carefully so as to not dislodge us both. When my face brushed his chest, my arms went around his neck.

"Now your legs," he advised against the top of my head.

For a second, I recalled the erection when I'd straddled him what felt like ages ago but had only been minutes. I held him tight around the neck, and my legs went around his waist and locked at his back. Tucked against him, we climbed. Or should I say, he did, and he wasn't even huffing by the time we hit the opening where Killian waited.

The prince didn't wait alone. We had an audience as we emerged on the first floor, the basement level being the one that had refused to open.

I disentangled myself from Levi and muttered, "Thanks." I then didn't say much as the Knight reported the rats and the destroyed elevator to the boss.

Hilda went on a rant. "How did those rodents get

in the building? Someone call maintenance."

"You need to do more than that. If they've infiltrated, we'll need an exterminator and also a team to go floor by floor looking for more threats," Levi interjected.

"Like I have the spare staff to do that," Hilda huffed. "We're already stretched thin."

"It has to be done," Levi stubbornly insisted.

Killian sidled close to me and murmured, "Think they'll notice if we slip away for that lunch?"

As if Levi heard, his head swiveled, and he fixed me with a glare, not the prince.

"Oh, he'll notice." As expected, Levi followed the moment we slunk off and headed for the door.

I wasn't actually hungry, but the idea of fresh air? Very welcome, along with the sunshine on my face.

We got our sandwiches, of which I only ate a few bites. Levi polished off the rest. Then we went with Killian to his hotel so he could go over the plans for the ball with a guest list that kept growing, as wannabe Cinderellas kept replying to the RSVP invitations that Killian swore he hadn't sent.

When Hannah and Gerome arrived at the suite for added protection—more Knights under Levi's watch—I took it as my cue to leave.

What I didn't expect?

Levi to accompany me.

5

"I don't need an escort," I repeated for the umpteenth time.

"I disagree." The same reply Levi gave each time I brought it up.

"You're going the wrong way," I stated when he turned in the opposite direction of the office. "The bureau's the other way."

"I'm dropping you at home."

"No, you aren't. My car's parked at the office."

"It will be fine overnight."

"It might, but how am I supposed to get to work tomorrow?" I pointed out the flaw in his plan.

Of course, he had an answer. "I'll pick you up before and bring you to meet with His Highness."

"Who says I want to go see Killian first thing?" I grumbled as I slumped in my seat.

"You're a princess. Shouldn't you be eager to meet a prince?"

"I am not a princess. I am from a lower middle-class family, born and raised in the Midwest. Since you're not familiar with the original Little Ash story, I'll let you know that Cinderella is a regular girl."

"Who, as part of her story, marries a prince and becomes a princess."

My lips twisted. "I am not getting married. Not to Killian, at least."

"Oh, you have another suitor in mind?" he asked casually.

"No." It might have emerged a tad vehemently.

"Why not?"

The question took me by surprise. "My personal life is none of your business."

He gripped the steering wheel tight as he muttered through a gritted jaw. "You're right, It's not."

Since he had opened that door, though… "Do you have a significant other?"

"No. Never will."

"Why not?" I asked, parroting him.

To which he aped me. "My personal life is none of your business."

For some reason, that made me giggle.

"What's so funny?" he groused.

"You and I. It's obvious we don't like each other."

"What makes you say that?"

"For one, you're always grouchy around me." I'd never seen the man smile.

"And you're snippy."

Was I? "I would have called it assertive, which for me is a big step. I used to be a regular doormat. Partly due to my upbringing, partly due to the Grimm Effect trying to shape me for its curse. It's not easy for me to say no to people."

"You seem to have no problem with me."

I couldn't help a grin. "I'm trying to be better about not letting people walk all over me, even if they're bigger and meaner."

"Bigger, yes, but I wouldn't say I'm mean." He sounded offended.

"I've read your file. You're not a man with much compassion."

"You seem to forget that I'm only called in to deal with dire situations, which usually require drastic measures. I'm the sword that cuts off the head of the monster so people like you can be safe."

"This mission must be a shock to the system then. No one to kill," I quipped.

"Yet," was his ominous reply.

"This is my place." I pointed to the old, converted Victorian with its three, sprawling stories.

"Big house for one person."

"Oh, it's not mine. I rent out the attic." As I hopped out of his SUV, I expected him to drive off, but, no, he followed me to the outdoor staircase that climbed at a steep angle.

"This must be hell in winter," he stated, as the structure groaned with every step he took.

"I salt the treads often."

I reached the landing, a cramped space that gave me a heck of a time when I had the delivery guys bring me a couch. I whirled to say thanks, only to find myself once more practically pressed against Levi's chest.

For some reason, my pulse raced. "Um, you can go now."

"I will after I check inside for any threats."

"What threats? I'm not the one in danger."

"We don't know that for sure. Or have you already forgotten what happened?"

"You're being dramatic. Those rats were an accident."

"And if they weren't?" his ominous rejoinder.

"The rats wanted Killian, not me. I'm a nobody."

"I highly doubt that," he muttered as he took my keys and reached around my frame to unlock the door.

We entered my place, and I called out a warning, "Dearest friends, I have a guest."

"Who are you talking to? Do you have a roommate?" He glanced around suspiciously.

"I have roommates of a sort." I crouched and held out my hand. "Izzy, come say hi."

My lizard waddled out from the bedroom where he'd probably been sunbathing on his perch.

As I scratched his head, I murmured, "This is Izzy, my iguana."

"You have a pet lizard."

"Yes." And then, because might as well warn him before he did something to upset me, "I also have mice."

"As pets?" he clarified.

I nodded. "Some neighborhood robins often visit as well. Then there's Roxanne, the raccoon, and her kits, Benjamin and Hank. I have a spider named Charlotte up there." I pointed out her web. "And a squirrel who comes around named Dory."

"Most people stick to cats and dogs."

I shrugged. "What can I say? I didn't actively go out and seek them. They kind of chose me."

"Like a real Cinderella." He shook his head.

His conclusion before I'd even mentioned my deer friends, Bobbi and Kira.

"Mind if I poke around?" he asked.

"Sure, but there's no one here."

"You can't be sure of that," he declared as he headed into my cramped bedroom.

I glanced down at Izzy, who flicked his tongue. "Actually, I can. My friends would have told me."

He emerged and frowned. "You talk to them?"

I shrugged. "Of sorts. I can more or less understand when they speak, and they understand me. Part of the Little Ash Girl gift."

"I thought it was a curse."

"Only parts of it, like the whole being mistreated and the fact one time I had a really old and gross prince try to force me to marry him."

"Killian isn't old and gross," Levi pointed out.

"What is your obsession with matchmaking?" I huffed. "For one, I just met the guy, two, not looking to settle down, and three, I don't need help getting a date."

"I'm not matchmaking."

"Then why do you keep mentioning it?"

His lips flattened. "Just doing my job and ensuring the prince isn't accosted when he least expects it."

My brows lifted. "Pretty sure I haven't done anything remotely close to accosting, nor do I plan to."

"Good." Levi glanced left and right. "I guess your place is secure enough."

"This is a safe neighborhood."

"Says everyone before something bad happens."

I cocked my head. "Are you always this pessimistic?"

"Yes. Don't forget, I know what people are capable of. I see the worst in humanity more often than most."

"You could change jobs."

"No, I can't. This is my cross to bear."

Why did he make it sound like his job as a Knight acted as penance?

"What time should I expect you in the morning?"

"What time can you be ready?"

"I get up at dawn. So any time after seven works for me."

"I'll be here."

"You'd better, or you're paying for my taxi," I warned.

"You have my number?" he asked as he stood on the threshold.

"Probably."

"Call if you hear or see anything out of the ordinary."

"I talk to and live with animals. Define ordinary."

Be still my heart, his lips quirked into an almost smile. "How about if anything scares you?"

"That covers too many things to count."

"I'll bet you're braver than you think."

A compliment? What was happening here? "I'd rather not test your confidence in that respect. See you in the morning, Sir Knight."

"My name is Levi." And with that, he left, yet the

scent of him lingered, and I must have stood there mooning because Izzy nudged my ankle.

I glanced down. "Yes, he's an interesting man."

Very. Also annoying. But handsome.

A good thing he wasn't a prince or I might have run into a problem resisting.

Just ask my dreams, where Levi knelt to put on my slipper and I didn't run away when he kissed me and... let's just say things got steamy.

Levi called Hannah. "The prince is secure for the night?"

"Yes, sir. He's currently reading a biography on Mötley Crüe, of all things."

"He's not your classic prince," Levi remarked. "No signs of trouble?"

"Nope. Gerome is patrolling the hallway while Sully and Pike are keeping an eye on the elevator and stairs via the cameras."

"Be sure to close the bathroom doors in the suite. Wouldn't want any rats to surprise you."

"We're on the twenty-fifth floor," Hannah pointed out.

"And? The rats we encountered today weren't the regular kind."

"Closing the shitter doors now." Three in total, given the prince had a two-bedroom suite with a living and dining room area.

"And the sliding glass door—"

"Already shut and locked. Windows are secured. The prince wasn't happy about keeping his bedroom door open for bedtime, but I told him it was that or I'd be sitting in a chair watching him sleep."

"He's definitely chafing at all the security," Levi agreed.

"More like he's not used to it. So I have to wonder, why now? You can't tell me this is over a treaty for honey and wine."

"My guess is he's the only eligible prince at the moment, making him in high demand, not just from potential Cinderellas but also every other Grimm story featuring a prince."

"Woe is the royal who has hundreds of women throwing themselves at him." Hannah chuckled.

"Not all of those tales are about marriage," he reminded. "We need to ensure he doesn't end up dead to satisfy a darker plotline."

"Understood, boss. When will you be getting back?"

"In the morning. I've got something I need handle. Call if anything happens."

"Will do. Night."

Levi hung up and reclined the seat in his SUV, which he'd parked in a pocket of shadow—that he created by busting a streetlight—watching the top floor of the house where Cinder lived. A woman not part of his mission, yet his gut insisted he stick close to her. She'd scoffed when he'd suggested the rat incident might not be about the prince but her. However, he had to wonder. Especially since Gerome found a basilisk skulking under her car.

Did Cinder have enemies?

If she did, they'd have to go through him.

With that final thought, he half shut his eyes and slumbered, doing his best to not think about the princess who wasn't meant for him.

6

I woke the next morning with a stretch and a smile. I sang as I showered and made breakfast. I fed my friends their breakfast before I ate my bowl of fruit smothered in thick cream.

Once dressed, I headed outside, just before seven, already planning to call a taxi if Levi wasn't—

He stood leaning against his blacked-out SUV parked in front of the house. Sunglasses covered his eyes, but I didn't need to see them to notice he looked as rigid as ever. Unlike the expression he wore in my dream last night. Remembering the things he'd done made my cheeks flush.

"You okay?" He pushed away from his car with a concerned expression.

"Yes, why do you ask?"

"Your face is awfully red."

It turned brighter at the fact he'd noticed. "Fine. I'm just hot."

"It's sixty-five degrees."

"Hot from cooking, um, porridge."

"Un-hunh." I couldn't tell if he believed my lie.

He opened the passenger door for me to get in and then slid behind the wheel.

"Anything happen overnight?" I asked.

"Nope."

"So the prince is...?"

"Fine."

Talkative sort in the morning. I glanced at Levi and noticed he wore a black T-shirt and jeans. Same as yesterday. Most likely he had a closet full of the same outfit. The scruff on his jaw was new, though. I don't think I'd ever seen him not clean-shaven.

"Anything planned for today?" I queried.

"Nope."

His one-syllable answers began to grate. "Can we swing by the bureau first? I don't have my suitcase." My briefcase of goodies, which I hoped to never have to use.

"Nope."

"Why not?"

"Because it's currently being fumigated."

Finally, more than a one-word reply.

He abruptly slammed on the brakes, and I would

have jolted harder if he'd not slapped an arm across my chest. On my boobs, I might add. He didn't do it to cop a feel, though.

I blinked at the family of swans, big and small, crossing the road. Given the stories only had adults, I couldn't help but murmur, "Are they multiplying?"

"Seems like."

Kind of gross, actually, since the swans used to be human but magic transformed them, which made me wonder about the chicks toddling along. Would they revert to human if the spell broke or remain birds forever since they were conceived in that shape? Either way, a good thing the government had a ban on killing swans.

The hotel appeared busy, not because of guests but the growing crowd of women, many dressed in ball gowns, some holding signs.

I'm your true love.

I'll put on the shoe.

Make me your princess.

"Jeez," I murmured. "The ball is still days away." And already these potentials were fully immersed in the curse. I understood the Grimm Effect influenced some of them to act this way. Still, some measure of self-respect should allow them to push back. You didn't see me doing my best to make Killian notice me.

I stepped out of the SUV and headed inside,

ignored by the crowd. Meanwhile, the truck got mobbed, blocking Levi from exiting. They banged the vehicle and pressed their faces to the window chanting, "It's the prince!"

A major groan of disappointment filled the air when Levi shoved open his door and stepped out.

As he headed for me, I walked into the lobby and promptly tripped...

...right into Killian's arms. So much for not throwing myself at the closest prince.

"Well, hello there. Guess you've changed your mind about falling for me," the prince teased.

I righted myself with a chuckle. "Dream on. They never mention in the stories how clumsy Cinderella can be."

Killian's hand on my arms lingered as he smiled. "If you ask me, flaws make a Cinderella more approachable."

"Where's your assigned Knight?" Levi snapped as he joined us.

Killian took a step back from me. "I'm afraid Hannah didn't manage to get on the elevator since it was rather full."

Levi looked like he might explode. "Your Highness knows he's not supposed to wander around alone."

"Calm down. Here she comes." Killian indicated as

the elevator opened and Hannah stalked out, looking ready to murder.

Levi intercepted her, and they bent heads to whisper.

"Uh-oh, I think you're in trouble," I murmured.

"One can hope." Killian didn't seem bothered one bit that he'd peeved the Knights. "I trust you're recovered from our mishap yesterday."

"Not a single scratch. And you?"

"Ready to see what the day has in store."

"Do we have a plan?"

"Food! The hotel, on my mother's orders, tried to feed me healthy stuff like spinach omelets made of egg whites with a serving of plain granola." Killian made a face.

"The horror," I agreed.

"My mother is convinced I need to eat better. Meanwhile, I think my figure is just fine." He spun for me and showed off his snug-fitting but worn jeans paired with a heavy metal T-shirt.

"Does this mean you're looking for a heart-attack breakfast?"

"Yes, do you know a place?" His expression lit up, and I couldn't help but smile.

"Indeed, I do. Miranda's Diner. Deep fried potatoes, real bacon, made-from-scratch waffles and pancakes. It's really quite good, if artery hardening. It's only a few blocks from here. Maybe a ten-minute stroll."

"The prince can't walk around in public," Levi stated flatly, having rejoined us without Hannah. "He'll be mobbed the moment he steps out that door."

I glanced through the glass and saw the women pushing against the police barricades.

"Which is why we'll go out the back," the prince exclaimed.

Before Levi could say no, Killian grabbed my hand and tugged me in his wake as he led me behind the reception desk, where the attendant gaped but didn't stop us.

Levi followed with a grumbled, "I am going on the record now and saying this is a bad idea."

"If you ask me, you're just grumpy because you're hungry." Killian teased the big man.

"I'm grumpy because this is foolish."

"We'll be fine. I have the best Knight, after all, guarding my back." Killian went through a door marked Employees Only, which led to a corridor with several closed doors. Killian didn't open any of the ones we passed, heading for the one at the far end marked Stairs – Basement.

"Do you know where you're going?" I asked as Killian led me at a quick trot down the steps.

"I studied the hotel schematics this morning. I'm

used to having to sneak out of places. Lucky for us, this hotel connects to the building behind it, which holds their laundry facility."

A glance over my shoulder showed Levi with his phone to his ear as he murmured, probably advising his team of our route. With an operation like this, agents would spread out rather than cluster around the target, moving ahead to watch for possible threats, guarding the rear.

The twist and turns we took had me confused. "Are you sure we're going the right way?"

"I memorized the blueprint, photographic memory being a skill of mine," Killian admitted. "Almost there." He yanked open a rusted metal door, and up some stairs we went, emerging in a storage closet then into a vast steamy place full of massive, industrial laundry machines.

While the workers gave us curious glances, no one impeded our path across to the door marked Exit. We emerged onto a sidewalk, and Killian gave me an exaggerated bow.

"If my lady would be so kind as to show the way..."

With Levi guarding our rear, I led us to the diner, which proved to be surprisingly empty, until I realized Gerome sulked in a corner. Mostly likely he'd thrown money at the patrons before tossing them out.

"I like to people-watch." Killian's claim led to us

sitting in a booth with a window. Levi remained standing by the long Formica counter, glowering.

"It's kind of exposed. Aren't you afraid of being recognized?" I asked, grabbing the plastic-coated menu.

"Let's be honest. Would anyone expect me to be here, dressed like this?" He indicated with a wave of his hands.

"Good point. However, if you're wrong, this won't be easy to extricate ourselves from." What could I say? Levi's caution might have rubbed off a bit on me.

"We'll be fine. Food and then to work. Your boss, Hilda, says you can run a background check on the guest list so we can weed out some of the troublemakers ahead of time. Maybe also pull any info you can on women affected by the Ash Girl curse, since they seem to be getting invitations that we didn't send."

"Wouldn't it be easier to just ban all the potential Cinderellas?" I asked.

"I would have, but Mum insisted some attend because, as she claims"—he raised his fingers to quote—"*I need grandbabies, and I won't have them be bastards.*"

My lips quirked. "And she's okay with the curse choosing your bride?"

He shrugged. "I mean they supposedly lived happily ever after."

"Wait, I thought you were against getting married, though."

"I am. But who knows? Maybe I'll come face to face with someone and be like, bam, she's the one."

"You believe in love at first sight?"

"First sight, email, phone call, tackle. You never know when it will happen." Killian rolled his shoulders.

"Shall we order? I am famished." My light breakfast hadn't stood the test of time, and the smell of deep-fried breakfast potatoes had me salivating.

Killian ordered the greasiest and unhealthiest stuff on the menu. Bacon, sausages, two waffles with whipped cream and strawberries, a side of potatoes.

I had the potatoes smothered in hollandaise with chunks of bacon and sausage. To those surprised I ate meat, being friends with nature didn't make me a vegan. Most of my friends were carnivores, and through them, I understood the cycle of life. Eat or be eaten. It was the way.

We stuffed ourselves. Well, the guys did. I managed about half and then carried my plate over to Levi and dropped it without a word, although he did quirk his lips. No surprise, he polished off the rest.

As I finished my coffee, the waitress, a sturdy gal of

later years, emerged carrying a tray and on it a massive pie. And I mean huge. It took up almost the entire surface of our table.

When she set it down with a heavy thump in front of us, Killian waved her off. "No thanks. We are quite stuffed."

"But it's a pie fit for a king," the waitress exclaimed.

"I'm not a king," he stated flatly, starting to rise, but me, I had my gaze glued to the heaving crust.

"Um, what's in the pie?" I asked as the surface began to crack.

"Step back!" Levi barked, yanking Killian away from the booth, but I had the waitress blocking me, so when the pastry exploded, the wings of the black birds baked in the pie buffeted me.

I threw my arms over my head, trying to protect my face, but I didn't have to worry because a familiar chest once more cradled me.

By the time the commotion died down, the waitress was in hysterics, probably because Gerome had a gun pointed at her while asking where she'd gotten the pie. Killian sat on a stool, eating a cookie, calm as could be. Levi glowered—no real surprise—and I started to laugh.

The big man glared and groused, "What's so fucking funny?"

"Considering there's a verse to the Sing a Song of Sixpence nursery rhyme that talks about someone losing their nose, this could have been much worse."

My comment didn't help. Levi barked, "Back to the hotel. But no heading out the front. Gerome has the SUV parked in the alley."

As we piled in, me in the back with the prince, Levi in the front with his gun in his lap while Gerome drove, Killian leaned over to whisper, "How did someone know I'd be at that diner?"

Not to mention have a pie with blackbirds already to go.

I didn't have an answer, but I just knew Levi would use this as an excuse to be even more strict.

I just didn't expect it to extend to me!

7

WE RETURNED TO THE HOTEL AND PULLED right into a loading dock door, meaning we avoided the crowd building out front. The curse worked overtime bringing Cinderella hopefuls, and I had to note that while single available princes were rare and often caused commotion when they appeared, I'd never seen this kind of frenzy before. It was further evidence of the curse morphing, becoming more intense. It made me worry what kind of darkness it might have in store.

Killian appeared amused, murmuring, "Satin, ribbon, and taffeta vendors must be raking in the dollars." This in response to the number of ball gowns being worn. Although I had to wonder how many of the women had been visited by a fairy godmother. Mine had not mentioned if she acted alone or if an army of them existed. How insane would that be to have dozens or hundreds of women waving wands around and transforming rags into dresses?

Once we entered the suite, I pulled out my laptop and began running the names on the guest list through the various databases I could access, looking for anyone with an arrest record. I also reviewed any pings on social media that might be cause for concern or indicate someone received one of the invitations that Killian hadn't sent. Of those I found, most appeared to be ordinary women, suddenly in the grips of the Little Ash curse.

Since the hotel chose to send up a lunch of soup and salad—on the queen's order—Gerome popped out and fetched us pizza. We weren't allowed to touch it until the Knights had a piece from each box. The pie surprise had left them even more alert.

As for me, the incident baffled. What did that rhyme have to do with the Little Ash curse? And why send it to Killian?

When I excused myself to use the washroom, as I washed my hands, the air sizzled and poof!

Fairy godmother stood there with me. A good thing the luxury hotel suite had a large bathroom or her wide skirt might have made things cramped.

"Hi, again," she chirped.

I leaned against the counter. "Back so soon? The ball isn't for a few more days."

She grimaced. "I'm aware. However, I thought I'd check in with you since the curse is nagging. One Godmother and hundreds of Cinderellas is making it hard for me to find time to eat and sleep."

Well, that answered my previous thought. "Do you have to grant all of them their wishes?"

"Only the authentic ones who are getting screwed like in the story. For example, I had one girl beaten black and blue by her mother for stating she'd be attending the ball and marrying the prince."

My mouth rounded. "That's awful."

"Agreed. Rather than dress her for the ball, I took her to another state and put her in a women's shelter. She won't make it back in time and will hopefully beat the curse."

"If it helps, I don't have any urge at all to throw myself at Killian." A relief. Yes, the prince could be charming, and most definitely handsome, but I felt nothing. The man invading my dreams wore a different face. At the same time, the Levi I interacted with when I closed my eyes resembled nothing of the man I knew in real life. The former actually smiled and liked me.

"Don't be so sure you're safe," Godmother warned. "You're one of the strongest pulls I have. So be careful. The Grimm Effect can be devious when it wants a certain outcome."

"I wish I understood why. Like, where did this magic come from? Why is it determined to make us live out fictional fairytales?"

"Can we really understand aliens?" her cryptic reply.

Before I could say anything else, someone knocked at the door. "Agent Jones, are you okay?"

"Fine," I loudly stated to appease Levi, even as I wondered why he'd be listening in on me in the first place.

"I hear you talking, yet your phone is out here."

"Just having a chat with my fairy godmother."

A reasonable answer, unlike his response, which involved kicking in the door.

Me and Godmother gaped at him and the gun he had pointed at her.

"Who are you? How did you get in here?" he barked.

"Once upon a time, people called me Agatha." The initial shock quickly wore off, and Godmother smiled. "And you are the boy who killed his father to escape his curse."

My eyes widened. "You killed your dad?" I wondered what tale that was associated with.

"He had good reason, dear girl. His father made a bargain with the Nixie in his swimming pool. Riches in exchange for the life born in his home, which turned out to be Levi. Unlike the original tale, where the father keeps the child far from the evil spirit, he tossed you in without a fight."

"How do you know that?" Levi barked. "That information is classified."

"Unfortunately, I know more than I ever wanted to." Agatha's lips turned down.

I glanced at Levi. "How old were you when your father gave you up?"

"Hours old, and he assumed I drowned, only the Nixie kept me alive. Took care of me. Raised me." He sighed. "But she wouldn't release me. Or should I say couldn't because of the terms of the deal brokered with my father."

My brain quickly did the math. "He had to die for you to go free."

"Yes."

"And in doing so, Levi broke the curse. The Nixie in the Pond hasn't afflicted anyone since," Agatha announced.

I blinked, trying to organize my thoughts on all this new information. For one, Levi wasn't like the other Grimm Knights, who were people caught by the curse, but in a good, not bad way, and had been turned into heroes, the kind that thrived on tracking, hunting, and saving the world. For another, Levi had broken his curse, cured the world of it. But how was that possible?

"Why did his refusal to follow the story break it, but others, like me, who didn't marry the prince, are still dealing with it?"

At my query, Agatha shrugged. "I'm sure there's a logical reason. However, I couldn't tell you what it is. I can only assume each story has a different condition. In his case, the story went off on a different tangent from the beginning and culminated in his father's death."

"Who died?" Killian suddenly appeared behind Levi. "And who is this? I didn't know we had a guest."

"Move back, Your Highness. I've yet to ascertain if this intruder poses a threat." Levi still had his gun pointed.

I slapped the barrel. "Stop it with the macho-man stuff. Agatha is my fairy godmother, and she wouldn't hurt me. She wouldn't hurt anyone."

"And yet I've inadvertently done so." She sounded so sad.

"It's not your fault the Grimm Effect forces you to act." I patted her arm.

"I'm so tired of it, though. We must find a way to put more of the stories back where they belong, in their books," Godmother emphatically stated.

A weird statement, but then again, could anything about this be categorized as normal?

"You're the fairy godmother?" For some reason, Killian retreated and made the sign of the cross.

Odd until the realization hit me. "He's afraid you're here to make us get married."

"Oh dear me no. I doubt that would break the Little Ash Girl curse." Godmother shook her head.

"What would, then?" I asked.

"I don't know. I mean jilting the prince obviously didn't. I've also seen some Cinderellas refuse to attend the ball, and that had no effect." Agatha tapped her chin.

"Someone has to die." Levi's stark assessment.

"Not everything needs to be killed," I retorted.

"And yet didn't killing the huntsman solve the Little Red Cap curse?" he countered.

"Yeah, I'd rather not have to croak," I huffed.

"Me, either," Killian interjected. "I'd marry before I went to that extreme."

"Agreed." I nodded in solidarity.

"Perhaps you can figure it out. In the meantime, I'm being tugged in so many directions. Until we meet again…" With that, Godmother faded from sight.

Levi glowered. "Fucking magic."

Whereas Killian looked pensive. "With the fairy godmother on our side, surely we stand a chance?"

I wouldn't be so sure. The last time she got

involved, I'd almost gotten forced into marrying an old pervert.

Killian and I spent the rest of that afternoon and early evening discussing the Little Ash curse in detail. I pulled up reports of previous incidences involving it.

It was Killian who pointed out, "I don't think it wants us to die." Indeed, we had a few cases where the prince killed his intended and one where the Cinderella slit the throat of her prince on their wedding night. None of those halted the recurring storyline.

"I guess that's a relief," I stated, "but, at the same time, brings us back to the dilemma of how to make it stop."

"Any Cinderellas get divorced?" Levi sat in the chair opposite me with a mug of coffee in hand, prepared by his bodyguards to ensure no foul play.

"Yes. Happens all the time once the fairytale magic and excitement wear off." People caught in the grip of the curse didn't realize how the Grimm Effect manufactured emotions.

"A dilemma for sure," he stated.

I packed up my laptop. "I should get home. My menagerie is probably getting hungry. Can someone call me a taxi?"

Hannah pushed away from the small kitchen bar in the main living area. "I'll drive you."

For a second, Levi opened his mouth, and I expected him to object. Instead, he nodded. "Take her straight home and make sure you see her inside."

I rolled my eyes as we left. "Is he always that paranoid?"

"No. But given this mission is different than usual, I'm thinking he wants to cover all his bases." Hannah offered an excuse.

"No one cares about me," I huffed.

"The prince might. You two seem to be getting along rather well. Guess it helps he's easy on the eyes," Hannah teased. The woman, who'd been caught in the Hansel and Gretel curse, had a naughty and sometimes dark sense of humor.

"We get along, but there's no spark."

"Spark is important," she agreed. "But sometimes not enough if the other person is stubborn."

I glanced at her. "You sound as if you speak from experience."

"Nope. I'm not cut out for a romantic relationship."

"I'd like one, but the moment guys realize I'm an actual Cinderella, they get all weird."

"Weird how?"

"I had one date who wanted me to wear these ridiculous stilettos so he could suck on the heel."

Hannah blinked at me as we reached the SUV. "Um, yeah, that would be a hard no from me."

"Ditto. Then there's the ones who think I will be their built-in maid. Also, a hard pass."

"Men are jerks."

"Agreed." I happened to glance up at the hotel, all the way up, where the lit penthouse windows were tiny specks of light, and yet I could have sworn I saw a shape in one.

Watching.

As we drove off, I said, "Mind swinging by the bureau so I can grab my car?"

"I take it Levi gave you a ride this morning from the office?"

"Actually, he gave me a lift from my place. He insisted on taking me home last night after the elevator fiasco."

"He did?" Hannah took her eyes from the road for a second.

"Yeah, even did a scout of my place, although I don't know for what. I don't have anyone targeting me."

"Levi doesn't do things without reason."

"If you ask me, he's convinced there's bad guys around every corner."

"In our line of work, that's often true." She

swerved to avoid the green goblin that darted across the road.

"The Little Ash Girl story doesn't have bad guys, just an evil stepfamily, and in my case, since I have no family left, it was coworkers."

"I'm sorry to hear that. How did your parents die?"

"Nothing fairytale related. Mom died having me, and Dad got caught in a house fire when I was at camp." A camp for misbehaved girls, which, no surprise, didn't apply to me. The irony being my stepsisters could have used it, but the fire took them, along with my stepmom and papa.

"My parents gave up trying to be responsible when I was young. At times, I'm pretty sure they didn't even remember they had a kid. Best choice I made for myself was running away. Scrounging for food is what led me to Gerome and eventually the witch."

I already knew he wasn't her brother, a variation on the tale. "You have to wonder how much the curse has to do with the tragic events that shaped some of us caught in the Grimm Effect," I mused aloud.

As she stopped for a red light, some pigs trotted across, followed by a bulky figure in a trench coat with impressive sideburns. I fired a quick text to the bureau to advise them of the location. We had someone attempting to track down the little pigs to keep them safe from the wolf that would try to eat them. They'd proven to be wily at hiding.

"Which is your car?" Hannah asked, pulling into the parking lot for my work.

I pointed to the small electric smart car, nearly identical to Belle's, as we'd bought the same model a year apart. Though Blanche hated them, I found them less scary than Blanche's motorcycle. The lot had quite a few vehicles still parked, which had me frowning. Had people already gone back to work?

"What's wrong?" Hannah asked as she parked beside my vehicle.

"I guess the exterminators got the job done fast."

"What exterminators?"

"The ones to handle the rats. Levi said I couldn't swing by the office this morning because of them.'

"Odd. I didn't hear or see anything when I popped by around lunch to grab something for the boss."

Why would Levi lie?

I headed for my car, and Hannah followed, for some reason dropping to her knees to check the undercarriage, poking her head inside, and then even popped the hood to glance at the engine.

"Good to go," she declared. "I'll be right behind you."

"You don't have to follow me home. I'll be fine."

"The boss gave me an order, and he'll skin me alive if I don't obey."

I sighed, but what could I do? I didn't want her to get in trouble.

The drive proved uneventful if I ignored the turtle doves that swooped past my windshield. Please don't tell me the Twelve Days of Christmas would become a thing.

My triplex appeared fine, but as expected, Hannah trudged up the stairs to do a cursory check. She met my friends, and Izzy fell in love after a good scratching.

"Guess I should head back," Hannah stated after feeding the mice some licorice she pulled from her pocket.

"I'll see you at the hotel sometime in the morning. I'm going to check in at the bureau first."

"Sounds good. Night, Cinder."

Hannah left, and I was alone but restless. Godmother, AKA call me Agatha, had dropped some interesting hints. As if she knew more about the curse than we did. Her comment about putting the stories back especially intrigued. It brought to mind the stories that had suddenly stopped reenacting. We'd assumed the curse tired of them, but the idea that they'd somehow been solved or, at best, re-enacted in a way so far from the original that it broke them, made a strange sense.

Could it be so simple? It seemed unlikely. After all, my simple solution of avoiding my prince hadn't solved the issue.

"What do you think, Izzy? How can I stop being a Cinderella?" I'd thought of changing my name but already knew most of the Little Ash heroines bore a different appellation. Killing didn't seem to solve anything. Nor did the prince marrying the wrong Cinderella. What did that leave?

I didn't know.

Since I'd eaten already, I simply had to prepare meals for my friends, hand feeding them while I told them about my day. When I readied for bed, I made sure all my doors and windows were locked, Levi's paranoia having rubbed off.

As I lay in bed, staring at my ceiling, I wondered what Levi did, an odd thought to have. We'd barely spoken all day, although I'd caught him looking in my direction more than once, usually frowning. It should be noted, I glanced over quite often too.

I couldn't deny being attracted to the man, even as I didn't like him. Bossy handsome jerk.

My tummy rumbled, and since I couldn't sleep, I got up and made myself a bowl of cottage cheese and berries. I'd sat on the couch to munch my snack when Izzy hissed and scuttled to her cabinet, which had a special hole to climb in. The mice who'd been hoping to lick my bowl scurried off with squeaks of *spider*.

"Guys, you shouldn't be like that. You'll hurt Charlotte's feelings."

Granted, I had issues the first time I met my eight-legged friend. Since that initial fright, I'd come to appreciate how she kept my place free of flies.

I scrolled my phone as I ate, intent on the screen, so when the couch cushion dipped, it took me by surprise.

But I didn't scream until I glanced and saw the spider sitting down beside me!

8

Remember the movie *Arachnophobia*? Remember the size of those spiders? Now imagine one in your apartment, spindly-legged, hairy, with a gaping maw big enough to swallow me.

I shrieked and saw my wide-open mouth replicated in its multi-faceted eyes. But worse? The mandibles that clacked as they tried to grab me!

I threw my bowl at its face and scrambled away. Not far because my small place didn't have anywhere to really go except the bedroom. But hiding in there would leave my other friends at risk. My phone sat across the room on the charger, meaning I couldn't even call anyone.

The eight-legged freak stalked me slowly, enjoying my fear, or so it seemed. It spat a gob of something gooey, which I barely managed to dodge. Before I could figure out a game plan, my door got kicked open, and in stormed Levi.

Looking more thunderous than a dark cloud and wielding a gun, he took one look at the threat and ditched the firearm for a sword he pulled from a sheath down his back. I'd not even known he carried one.

With blade in hand, Levi partially crouched and kept his gaze on the spider, which moved more cautiously with a real threat to face.

He didn't look at me as he muttered, "Before I slice it to pieces, can I assume this isn't one of your friends?"

Had the curse giganticized my sweet Charlotte? "Um…" I glanced to the ceiling with its little web and saw Charlotte quivering in a corner of it. "Definitely a foe."

"Permission to kill?"

Since when did he ask? "Squash it!" And my friends thought I didn't have a single cutthroat gene. This was one time I fully advocated for the killing of a living thing.

The one thing I didn't take into account?

The mess.

As legs were severed, each spewing nasty glowing green ichor, my place got goobered. Slime spewed from each stump, and the spider retaliated by shooting balls of slimy thread. Splat. Ick. Gross.

Despite standing out of the way, I couldn't avoid getting covered in the gore from the fight, and by the time it finished, with Levi victorious over the corpse of the massive spider, my place had been ruined.

I hadn't fared much better.

I blinked my sticky lashes in shock, which led to Levi barking, "Cinder, are you all right?"

"Do I look all right? I've been slimed." And it stank.

"You're not injured, though?"

I shook my head.

"Good. But I know someone who's going to get a verbal beating. Fucking Hannah. She told me she checked your place."

"She did." I jumped to her defense. "I don't know where the spider came from. Suddenly, it was just sitting beside me as I ate my cottage cheese." In that moment it hit me. "Little Miss Muffet."

"What?"

"It's a nursery rhyme." I frowned. "Although the spider wasn't that big in the poem and has nothing to do with my story curse at all."

"Wait, since when is the Grimm Effect reenacting poems?"

"It might be," I cautioned. "We shouldn't jump to conclusions from a few incidents."

"How many will it take?" he drawled. "Or are you waiting for one of them to kill you?"

I wanted to argue, but I had nothing. "I don't know what's going on."

"What's going on is you're being targeted."

"Which makes no sense unless..."

"Unless what?"

"The Grimm Effect somehow thinks I'm going to ruin the Little Ash tale. In which case, it would make sense for it to get rid of me."

His brow arched. "I doubt the Grimm Effect is sentient enough to care about a single person."

"We don't know enough about it to say anything for sure, but I don't know what else makes sense."

"I do. Hundreds of wannabe Cinderellas who see you as a threat on their pathway to marrying a prince."

"That's just silly. I don't want to marry Killian."

"They don't know that. Could even be the curse is trying to convince you that you should."

"It will have to try harder," I huffed. "I am not marrying anyone unless it's for love. The real kind," I emphasized. "Not some magical spell that makes me think I am."

"How would you ever know the difference?"

"I just would." I had to believe that.

"You've been in love before?"

I shook my head. "No, but I've read enough

romance novels to know how it feels. How your heart flutters when they're near or you think of them. How your toes curl when they kiss you. How your dreams and thoughts are consumed."

A moue of disgust twisted his features. "Sounds unpleasant."

"It's the best thing in the world if you can find it." I'd seen the transformation in my good friend Blanche, from grouchy to happy.

"Must be nice for those who can find it."

"It could happen to you."

"Doubtful. As you've stated before, I am a killer, and the kind of women that attracts… Let's just say I'd rather be alone."

I almost opened my mouth to say he underestimated his appeal, but then that might lead to me saying something dumb like how good-looking I found him, and sexually appealing, plus kinder than expected. Not to mention brave, rushing in to rescue me.

"Wait a second, how come you knew I needed help? Are you spying on me?" I glanced around for cameras.

"Uh, well, um, I might have, kind of, um, been staked out watching your place."

I narrowed my gaze on him. "Why?"

"Because my gut told me to."

It made me think of his appearance that morning. He'd since changed and shaved, which led to a light bulb moment. "You were here last night too!"

"And if I was?" he huffed. "You should be glad I listened to my instincts, or you'd be cocooned and marinating for the spider." He waved a hand at the body, and I shuddered.

"Fine, you were right, and I'm glad you were nearby, but you could have told me."

"What would that have accomplished?"

"You could have slept on my couch instead of your car."

He grimaced. "I think my SUV is more comfortable." He might have a point given my love seat wouldn't accommodate his length.

"You must have been close to have heard the commotion."

"Close enough. Luckily you scream pretty loud. Surprised you didn't shatter a few windows."

I arched a brow. "Not all of us are warriors. And I hate bugs."

"Says the woman who is friends with a spider."

"A little one who wouldn't hurt—" I couldn't say fly so substituted with, "Me."

Levi glanced around. "Your place is a mess."

"I'm aware. This is going to take forever to clean." I sighed.

"You're not cleaning this. This is now a crime scene, which means we need to call the bureau for a team to bag, tag, and document."

"Think they'll let me stay while they handle it?" I already knew the answer. Protocol stated people had to vacate the premises of a crime scene.

"No."

"Where am I supposed to go?" I said then immediately snapped my fingers. "I'll call Belle. She has a spare room at her place."

"You're not staying with Belle." A flat reply.

"Yeah, well, I am not paying for a hotel that won't let me bring my friends." With the threat gone, the mice emerged, their pink noses twitching from their openings in the walls, which looked like doors since I'd drawn around them, giving them frames, and even fake windows with flower boxes.

"Hold on, you're bringing mice with you?"

"Not just the mice. Izzy and Charlotte, too, if she'll leave her web."

For some reason, Levi sighed.

"What?" I exclaimed. "Why do you look so annoyed?"

"Because I am not an animal, or arachnid, kind of guy."

"I don't understand."

"You're obviously being targeted, princess, which

means you need protection. Since we're both working the same mission with the prince, it makes the most sense that you stick close to me."

I blinked. Digested his words then gasped, "You expect me to stay with you?"

"I've got a suite at the hotel, one floor below the prince. It's got two queen beds so no worrying about your virtue."

"Why can't I get my own room?"

"Because I can't spare an extra guard."

"Killian has an extra bedroom in his penthouse suite." I couldn't have said why I mentioned it.

Levi's expression went several unhealthy shades of red and purple before he growled, "No."

"Excuse me? Why not? It would make sense to have us both in the same place, seeing as how we both need protection."

"It might make the curse harder to manage. Unless you want to marry the prince?" For some reason he sounded angry saying it.

"No, I don't want to marry him. Add to that, if there was concern about the curse, then why would anyone put him with me as our liaison in the first place?"

"It wasn't my idea," he snarled. "I argued against it, but the director overruled me."

"I'll bet that made your bossy butt happy." My tart reply.

"Why must you be so difficult?"

"Because spending time with you is a trial," I grumbled. "Do you think I enjoy arguing? I'm a happy person. A simple person. Not a person who deals with monster spiders and rat armies in elevators or black birds baked in a pie."

"Well, get used to it for the next little bit because I have a feeling it's only going to get worse."

"You really need to start playing ominous music when you make those kinds of dark declarations."

He glowered.

"Actually, that expression works too."

"Pack a bag while I call for a crew to dissect the crime scene."

"Can't I shower first?" Yes, I whined.

"No. We don't want to disturb any of the pipes in case the spider used one to squeeze its way in."

"You saw the size of it. No way it came up through my tub."

"Seeing as how spiders that size don't exist, I wouldn't rule it out. Especially since your windows and door were shut. Now, no more arguing. Pack."

"Grumpy butt," I muttered as I went into my room. Despite what he said, I did change clothes, dropping my slimy nightgown to the floor and then using a towel to mop my face and hair as best I could. The mice were already at work, packing my suitcase, not just with clothes for me, but with supplies for them and Izzy too.

Apparently, Charlotte would be staying, tucked up in the rafters. Levi's murder of the other arachnid freaked her out. Understandable.

I emerged from my bedroom with my suitcase in hand, mice perched on my shoulders and in my pockets. By the door stood Izzy, who flicked his tongue at me.

"Yes, you're coming too," I assured him.

Levi stood in the kitchen area with his phone to his ear, but he put it away upon seeing me.

"Give me the case." Levi snared my suitcase, leaving me free to scoop my lizard. We then marched down the stairs to his SUV just as flashing lights arrived, spilling the bureau's forensics team. While crimes involving humans still required police to do their own investigation, cases involving otherworldly creatures, such as the spider, went through a different processing, a magical version conducted by witches. Surprised we employed sorceresses? You shouldn't be since not all magic wielders turned out bad.

I headed for my car, only to have Levi snap, "Where do you think you're going?"

"To the hotel. Duh." It slipped out.

"My car is that way." He pointed to the large SUV.

"I want to have mine handy."

"I can't protect you if we're in separate vehicles."

I took a mulish stance. "I am not being left without transportation again."

He glared at me as if he could bully me into compliance. He'd obviously not met the people in my life who thought they could walk all over me.

Rather than pointlessly argue, I simply got in my car and started it. The mice scampered off to their spots. Orville liked riding on the front dash. Rosy got carsick and usually huddled on the mat in the backseat. The rest liked to cuddle in the cup holder. As for Izzy, he usually took the passenger seat, but this time, he scooted into the back.

I craned and frowned. "Everything all right?"

Tongue flick. *Fine.*

Creak.

The car sank as Levi sat in the passenger seat.

I blinked. "Um, what are you doing?"

"Riding with you."

"But what about your car?"

"Gerome can get it in the morning."

"You can't seriously think I'm going to be attacked again tonight."

"You've already had two incidents today."

"We don't know the pie was intended for me. After all, it was baked for a king."

"I swear, if you don't shut up..."

"You'll what?" I sassed.

To my shock, he suddenly gripped me by the head and dragged me close for a kiss!

9

THE KISS LASTED ONLY SECONDS.

Long enough to steal my voice.

Long enough to scramble my thoughts.

Long enough to cream my clean undies.

Short enough that I almost wondered if I imagined it but for the tingling of my lips and the smug look on his face.

Rather than ask why he did it, I drove. Drove and wondered how to ask why he'd kissed me. The most basic answer could be that he found me attractive. No doubt he'd been aroused when I'd fallen atop him in the elevator. Then again, most men would have been hard-pressed to not respond, given how intimately I'd straddled him. However, the way he spoke to me, and acted, didn't jibe with how a man usually behaved around a woman he liked.

"It meant nothing." He spoke suddenly.

"What didn't?" I played dumb.

"The kiss. It was stupid. I shouldn't have done it, but I had no idea how else to get you to stop talking."

"You could have asked."

He snorted. "As if that wouldn't have unleashed a storm."

"You shouldn't be kissing a woman unless it means something." It might have emerged a tad miffed. So much for briefly thinking he might have been overwhelmed by passion.

"It won't happen again."

"Good." I lied. I'd enjoyed the brief embrace but, given his reaction, had to wonder, was the magic in the curse trying to drag him in? How would he fit into the Little Ash Girl story?

"When we get to the hotel, you'll drive into the loading dock like we did this morning." He turned businesslike, and I wanted to scream.

I wanted to talk about the kiss that he claimed meant nothing, because for me it changed everything.

Before I'd ignored the flutters when he appeared. The dreams featuring him. The racing pulse. The attraction.

But now, with my lips and other parts of my body yearning for more, it hit me.

I like him.

Liked him, as in, how a woman liked a man. Only he'd already made it clear he didn't date or want to settle down. As for me, I wasn't into casual flings.

"Princess." He snapped his fingers in front of my face.

"What?"

"The light is green."

"Oh." I drove in silence, but he suddenly got talkative.

"Are you reliving the attack?"

"No." The truth.

"You don't have to worry. I'll be keeping a close eye on you."

How close? "You're not going to make me use the bathroom with the door open, are you?"

"No. But someone will be close by in case you yell."

"Not you." Bodily functions might be normal, but that didn't mean I wanted anyone listening while I tinkled or worse.

"If I'm not around, someone else will be."

"Shouldn't I share a room with Hannah, you know, her being a woman and all?"

"Hannah doesn't like to share, and her room only has a king-sized bed."

"Oh."

"I know that kiss might make you think otherwise,

but you don't have to worry about your virtue. I will treat you with the utmost respect."

Pity.

Wait, did I say that out loud? A glance showed him looking out the window.

My shoulders relaxed. What was wrong with me?

The hotel loading dock door somehow knew to open as I neared. I pulled inside to see Hannah waiting.

She took one look at my gummed hair and probably still sticky face and whistled. "Hot shit, look at you."

I grimaced. "I'm a mess."

"We'll get you cleaned up," she promised. "Follow me."

"Just a second. I need to gather my friends." Izzy crawled into my arms, while the mice raced up my sleeves to ride on my shoulders.

To her credit, Hannah didn't say a word about my menagerie. She led the way to a service elevator that took us to our floor. When she stopped in front of a door, Levi barked, "She's staying with me."

Hannah whirled around so fast I worried about whiplash.

"With you?" she questioned.

"I have two beds." Said almost defensively.

Hannah glanced at me then Levi before she

drawled, "Good point. I'm a rough sleeper. I might kick Cinder if we shared."

The door for Levi's suite proved to be farther down the hall and opened onto a decent-sized space. A corner unit with windows on two sides and the promised two beds. It also had a small kitchenette, a couch, and even a round table with two chairs. Homey.

The mice cheered as they scampered off to explore. Izzy turned his nose up at the carpet.

"I know, buddy. You prefer wood flooring. This is temporary."

Hannah and Levi whispered at the door before he said more loudly, "Why don't you shower. I'll be in the hallway if you need me."

"Oh yes!" I might have yelled it a little too happily.

The door to the room shut, and I stripped, quickly immersing myself under the hot spray. Spider goo sluiced from my flesh, and I sighed in relief, especially since it didn't seem to have left behind any skin irritation. Since I had my eyes closed, I didn't immediately notice the tub filling with water. When it swirled around my ankles was when I took note. I must have accidentally stepped on the pressure plug.

The murky water, covered in a layer of suds, meant dipping my hand in to swish around looking for the round metal cap so I could press it. Something brushed past my fingers and startled me enough I jerked, which, in turn, unbalanced me, and I landed with a splash on my ass. The jolt whooshed my breath, meaning I didn't even manage an audible squeak.

As I pushed to stand, something slid by my hand again, and on reflex, I closed my fingers around it. I lifted it from the water to blink in surprise at the fish I'd caught. A squirmy little bugger that flapped its mouth open and shut before chomping me!

"Ow!" I dropped the fish and barely had time to wonder where it went after it splashed before the door slammed open.

Levi stood on the threshold, once more gun in hand, expression slightly crazed as he barked, "What is it?"

I scrambled from the tub and pointed to the water. "There's a fish."

"A fish?" he repeated, his expression confused.

"Yes, a fish in the tub. It bit me!" I held out my hand to show the red mark.

Despite his frown, he knelt by the side and reached in, finding the plug, and with a suctioning noise, the water began to drain. Even before it fully evacuated, the fish appeared, flopping on the bottom, orange-scaled and kind of fat. It reminded me of an oversized goldfish.

"What the ever-loving fuck?" he muttered as he reached in to snag it by the tail.

"What are you going to do with it?" I asked, standing there shivering despite the towel I'd wrapped around myself.

"Gonna save it for the bureau." He plopped it into the sink, which he filled with water. "Finish your shower."

"I'll wait."

"You're covered in soap. Rinse," he snapped.

"I will once you leave."

"Ain't happening, princess. Or are you hoping for an alligator next time?"

I glanced at the empty tub. Would the Grimm Effect be so savage? I didn't know what to think anymore. "Don't peek." A dumb thing to say given A) he'd already seen my naked bits, B) I kind of wanted him to look and admire, C) he obviously wasn't that interested, given he'd not met my gaze since entering.

I placed the damp towel on the bar, and the curtain rustled as I went back into the shower. Clear plastic on the inside, a filmy white fabric on the outside. He technically couldn't see much even if he did look, which he didn't. I'd have known since I kept turning my head to see.

The shower remained hot, but I shivered a bit inside. What was happening to me? Another nursery rhyme at play? I knew of one from when I was young, One, Two, Three, Four, Five. The short sing-along poem spoke of catching a fish and letting it go because it bit. Just like what happened to me.

"You okay in there, princess?"

"Yup. Done. Turn around while I grab a towel."

His broad back faced me as I slid back the curtain. My damp towel didn't help my chill; however, I wasn't rude enough to grab the other, as he would need it when he bathed. Levi also had some spider gore to deal with. Not as much as me, which made no sense since he'd been the one slicing.

A peep at the sink showed the giant fish sulking at the bottom, and I'd swear it glared at me as its mouth opened and closed. At least it didn't have razor-sharp teeth.

My bag of clothes sat by the vanity, on the other side of Levi. "Could you step out while I dress?"

"Leave the door open."

So much for having any privacy. At the same time, I appreciated the fact he wanted to protect me. At the same time, that appreciation wouldn't last if he insisted on standing over me while I peed.

I dressed quickly in leggings and an oversized sweatshirt. My hair I wrapped in the towel to sop up most of the moisture. I kept my feet bare and emerged into the room to find Levi pacing, his posture tense.

"Sorry I freaked out about the fish."

He whirled and growled, "Don't you dare apologize. Something weird is going on, and that gives you the right to be upset."

"Weirder than me talking to mice?" I tried to make light of the situation before immediately frowning. "That's odd."

"What is?"

To be sure, I returned to the bathroom and stared at the fish.

It glared back.

"I don't think it's sushi material," he drawled at my back.

"I wanted to check something."

"Dare I ask what?"

I turned to see him standing close, close enough I had to crane to see his face. "It doesn't speak."

"It's a fish. Kind of normal."

I shook my head. "Most animals have the ability to communicate, just not in a language most understand. It's how I can speak with my mice and Izzy and all my other friends. But this fish..." I waved my hand. "It's blank."

Judging by his expression, I had his interest. "What do you mean by blank?"

"It's not exuding any thoughts or emotions. As if it

doesn't have a mind. Or if it does, not one that projects."

"Could be it's not a thinker."

"Everyone has thoughts. Everyone feels something, whether it be joy, annoyance, sadness, anger. My mice right now are excited about the new room. Izzy is disgruntled by the carpet, which he claims smells. But this fish has nothing."

"What do you think it means?"

My lips pursed before I blurted out, "I think it's not real."

He arched a brow. "It's real. I touched it. So did you."

"Sorry, that's not the right word. More like it exists but isn't an actual fish."

"Then what is it? A dog?" his sarcasm clear.

"I think it's a golem."

"A giant mud monster?" This time his query shone with incredulity.

"A golem is a magical construct that mimics a living thing. Traditionally, it's a giant, but technically, it could be anything."

"So the curse is now making fake living things?"

I shrugged. "I don't know. What I do know is if it starts making something out of nothing, we're going to have problems. Big ones."

"As if we don't already."

"You're not seeing the bigger picture. Right now, when people are transformed, they still retain some of their humanity, along with whatever morality they followed in their pre-curse life. For example, just because someone becomes a wolf doesn't mean they'll automatically start killing." Aidan, Hood's boyfriend, was a good example of a wolf with a moral code. "A human, even transformed, is afraid of pain and tries to avoid death. But imagine something like that fish, no compassion, no emotions whatsoever. That kind of blank slate would be capable of anything, even the most depraved act, because it would feel nothing."

His lips stretched into a thin line. "You're talking about sociopath golems."

"Yes. If the curse were to start creating them and setting them loose, can you imagine the havoc they'd cause?"

"Assuming the Grimm Effect can do something large-scale, it would be bad," he agreed. "However, given it's always used magic to create elements for its curses, this isn't really new. I mean look at places like Regent Park and the trees that sprouted overnight. Trees are living things."

He raised a valid point. I chewed my lower lip. "I don't know why, but this feels different."

"I agree, and this is why you and I will be joined at the hip until the danger passes."

"What of the prince?"

"The other knights can handle him."

"And just how long do you plan to remain glued to me?"

"As long as it takes."

I arched a brow. "Why, Levi, are you proposing 'til death do us part?" I teased, but his face... Oh my goodness, his face. It turned red, bright red, and he stammered.

"I won't let you die. And as for the length of time, most likely, once the ball is over, things will go back to normal."

I snorted. "As if there's such a thing anymore." Mind you, I'd hardly lived in a world pre-Grimm. I was very young when it hit and so never knew that other time before we had to worry about magic.

"I will keep you safe, princess."

"I know you will."

But while he guarded my wellbeing, who would protect my heart?

10

Awkward. The only word to use when getting ready to sleep alongside the man who made my pulse thump something fierce.

Actually, it might be better described as frustrating. I lay in the bed staring at the ceiling because I couldn't help but think of Levi. Dumb, I know. With all the things I should be worrying about, whether he liked me or not shouldn't be one of them. As a grown woman, why did I care? Not to mention, we were completely mismatched. Me, gentle and nonviolent, versus his brusque, let's-kill-things-first attitude.

I'd assumed he'd fallen asleep until he said, "You don't have to worry."

"Who says I'm worried?"

"You're still awake."

"So are you," I pointed out.

"I don't need much rest."

"Who says I do?"

He grumbled, "Is there a reason why you don't like me?"

The query floored. "Why would you think I don't like you?"

"For one, I'm the only person you argue with."

Valid, so how to explain? "You are, but in my defense, you're bossy."

"So is Hilda, and yet you do your job without argument at work."

"That's different."

"Not really. This is still work."

"For you maybe, but for me, this is very personal." I paused then added. "I'm an office agent so not usually the one dealing with the side effects of curses. Not since the ball decades ago has it ever focused on me."

"That must be disturbing."

"Very. Mostly because I don't understand what it means."

"We'll figure it out."

I snorted. "Scientists and everyone with a brain cell has been trying since the Grimm Effect emerged to find answers. We're still waiting."

"I think it's obvious the curse is attempting to murder you."

"But why? I'm not even a contender for the prince's hand."

"Maybe it wants you to be. Would it be so bad? Killian seems a decent sort." His voice turned gruff as he said it.

"He's not so bad. However, like I said before, I want love."

"Even if it means your life?"

I thought about that before shaking my head on the pillow, only to realize he couldn't see the motion. "I'm a person who wants her happily ever after but on my terms, not because of some curse. I want a man to fall in love with me, for me. Not because of magic."

"Some people say love is its own form of spell."

"Do you think love is magic?"

"I don't think about love at all." A flat reply.

"Surely you've cared for someone in the past."

He made a noise. "Yeah, and it was a mistake."

"Oh, what happened?" Yes, I pried, but given he seemed willing to talk, I wanted to understand him better.

"Let's just say it didn't work out. Before you ask, she decided I was too emotionally detached. She wasn't wrong."

"Then it wasn't love."

"How can you be sure?"

"Because when you love someone, you do everything in your power to make them feel special. You understand them and their needs. You want them to be happy."

He didn't say anything for a second, and I thought he'd fallen asleep, only for him to say, "But what if that person doesn't reciprocate?"

"Then perhaps they weren't the right person after all."

Funny how his words and my own advice applied to me. Levi didn't see me as a possible love interest no matter how he made me feel. Could it have been love? Most definitely, but I wouldn't chase after a man who made it clear he had no interest.

The room went quiet after that, and I eventually fell asleep, only to wake up to tiny feet scratching and scampering. I sat up and, in the faint light from the window, discerned my mice racing up the bed frame and across the mattress to the nightstand to climb onto the digital clock with its red numerals.

Since I didn't want to wake Levi, I didn't speak. Even more oddly, neither did the mice. It bothered to see my little friends sitting there swaying above a time of 12:56 a.m.

Despite me not making a sound, Levi suddenly asked, "What's wrong?"

"The mice are acting odd."

I heard the rustle of sheets as he slid out of his bed. "Odd how?"

"They just ran up to the clock. I think they might be sleepwalking but as a group?" I ended my statement on a query.

He groaned. "Oh for fuck's sake."

"What?"

"Don't tell me you don't know? Hickory, dickory, dock."

I could have slapped my sleep-muddled mind. "You think they're caught in the rhyme."

"Guess we'll find out in two minutes."

I didn't expect him to perch on my bed to watch with me as the numbers flipped to 12:59. Having him so near made me shiver, and he noticed. His arm went around me, tucking me into his side.

"You're okay, princess."

Should I explain that lusty thoughts and not fear made me quiver when he got near?

Nope. I snuggled closer, inhaling the scent of him.

His arm wrapped around me far enough his hand rested on my outer thigh. The thumb lightly stroked, and that didn't help my awareness of him.

At exactly one o'clock, the mice ran down and scurried off to the nest they'd made. But Levi didn't move.

It led to me quipping, "See. Not all the rhymes are deadly."

"Don't be so sure of that."

"My mice wouldn't hurt me."

"Wasn't talking about them," he muttered.

I shifted sideways so I could see his strong profile. "Guess we could go back to bed."

"Yeah." One word and yet, as his gaze met mine, he didn't leave.

I reached up to lightly touch his cheek.

He inhaled sharply. "Princess..." He had a warning tone in the word.

"I'm not a royal."

"Close enough."

I shifted until I knelt beside him, aligning our faces. "Do you like me?" I asked bluntly, the darkness giving me the courage to ask.

"Of course. You're a good agent."

"I'm not talking like me as in work," I grumbled. "I mean like me, like me."

"That wouldn't be appropriate."

I sighed. "I guess that's my answer." I slumped and looked away. To my surprise, calloused fingers lightly gripped my chin so I faced him once more.

"It's not appropriate, but at the same time, I can't seem to help myself."

Wait, was he saying—

Rather than ask for clarification, I chose to be bold and pressed my mouth to his then gently slid them in a soft kiss.

He froze, only for a second, before his arms wrapped around me and he returned the embrace, his mouth hard and commanding. Coaxing as well. My lips parted to deepen the kiss, our tongues twining, as did our breaths.

I found myself in his lap, straddling him, cupping his cheeks and kissing him as if he were the most decadent dessert. In a sense, he was. I'd never tasted something so intoxicating. Kissing him woke all of my nerve endings and had me tingling in a way I'd never imagined.

He groaned against my mouth. "We shouldn't be doing this."

"Why not?" I whispered before I nipped his lower lip.

"We're coworkers."

"There's no rule against it."

He growled. "There should be since I find you distracting."

"Thank you." I took it as a compliment to hear the stoic Levi admit I made him weak.

"You don't want to be involved with me."

"Probably not," I agreed. "But I can't seem to help myself."

"You're making this hard."

I squirmed on his lap and agreed. "Indeed, I am." His erection bulged against my bottom, and I wanted nothing more than to strip his clothes and see it.

My hands went to his shirt.

"Princess, we really shou—"

"Oh shut up and kiss me, Levi."

I'd shocked him. Shocked myself too. But in good news, he didn't dump me from his lap. He lay me on the bed and covered my body with his, the weight somewhat dispersed by his forearms as he held himself over me, kissing me while grinding against me.

The clothes separating our flesh did nothing to diminish the sensation. He rubbed, and I gasped. He rotated his hips, pressing that hidden erection against the core of me. My fingers dug into his shoulders as my hips thrust.

He uttered a low rumbling noise as he kept a steady thrusting rhythm that had me panting and holding on to him.

His kiss stole all the sounds I made. And I made quite a few as he brought me to the peak. He even caught my cry of pleasure as I came.

Came simply from rubbing.

He shuddered a second later and then brusquely said, "I need to use the washroom."

I might have been more offended but for the wet

spot that had seeped through his track pants to leave me slightly damp.

He'd come too.

A man with his rigid control had lost it to me.

When he emerged from the bathroom, pants changed, he didn't say anything but crawled into his bed.

I might have been offended, only I knew he probably suffered from embarrassment. I'd read enough romances to know how men felt about their virility. Did I leave him to wallow by himself, though?

Nope.

I crawled from my bed to his, ignoring Levi's rough, "What are you doing, princess?"

"Snuggling. It's what I like to do after sex."

"We didn't have sex." His voice sounded raw.

"Oh yes we did, so now you have to cuddle me."

"Have to?"

"Yes." I scooched into him until my butt hit his groin. Rather than protest further, he threw his arm over me and tucked me closer.

That night I didn't dream of Levi. I didn't have to because we stayed tucked together all night long.

Until a pounding at the door in the morning.

11

I MIGHT HAVE BEEN INSULTED AT THE ABRUPT way Levi left the bed, only he pulled the covers over me and dropped a kiss on my lips before stalking to the door to bark, "What is it?"

Hannah, on the other side, sounded slightly amused as she said, "We have a situation upstairs."

Those words galvanized me. I hopped out of bed and scrounged in my bag for clothes as Levi yanked open the door. "Report."

Hannah walked in, and I had to wonder if she guessed right away that we'd slept together. Maybe not seeing as how both beds were mussed and we were both clothed.

I paused on my way to change in the bathroom at what she said.

"A Cinderella potential managed to pose as hotel

staff. She delivered the prince's breakfast and now won't leave unless he asks her to marry him. She even brought a glass slipper so he can do it properly."

"Why is this even an issue? Toss her out." Levi offered a simple solution.

Hannah shook her head. "Would love to. However, she's holding a knife to her throat and says she'll slit it if the prince doesn't comply."

I winced. The optics would be horrible if that happened.

"For fuck's sake." Levi raked his fingers through his hair. "Give me a second to change."

"Will do, boss." Hannah finally looked at me directly, and her wide smile went well with her chirped, "Judging by the hair, I'd say someone had a good night."

Could she tell Levi and I had fooled around?

"Comfy bed," I mumbled, wondering if my cheeks turned red because I certainly heated at the insinuation.

"If you're done giving me your update..." Levi's statement held a warning tone.

"That's all for now. I'll head back upstairs and wait for you, but hurry. The prince isn't happy."

The door closed, and Levi muttered, "Goddammit. Not how I wanted to start my morning."

"And how were you planning to start it?" I chirped.

He cast me a dark look. "What do you think?"

"I think," I said, my cheeks hot as I stripped my shirt under his avid gaze, "that I can't wait until tonight."

He uttered a long-suffering groan as I dressed in front of him with absolutely no shame. There was something powerful and heady about his smoldering interest. Seeing how his pants tented roused my own carnal hunger. And when he closed the distance between us to drag me into his arms for a kiss? I just about came again. The man knew how to get me humming.

When he broke the kiss, it was with a muttered, "Way too distracting. I'm getting dressed in the bathroom."

"No fair. Don't I get a peek, too?" I pouted.

"We don't have time for this right now, princess."

At the downturn of my lips, he softened to add, "I will make time later."

"Yay." I might have clapped my hands.

Which led to more muttering on his part and a slam of the bathroom door. I spent that scant moment feeding my friends from the stash I'd brought. I'd have to order some room service to ensure they had ample supplies in case I couldn't pop back in for a while.

By the time Levi emerged, I was doing the morning pee dance. He took one look at me and pointed to the bathroom. "Go."

"Don't listen," I exclaimed as I went and emptied my bladder, because nothing screamed sexy like, *Hear me pee!*

I emerged, teeth brushed and face washed, to see him typing on his phone.

"Ready," I announced.

"Good." He tucked his phone away. "We'll take the stairs."

"Do you think the elevator is unsafe?"

"I'm not taking chances."

The single flight didn't tax me at all, and as we neared the prince's suite with its door wide open, I spotted Gerome skulking just outside.

"I assume the situation is unchanged," Levi asked as we neared.

"Woman's nuts," Gerome muttered.

The woman also turned out to be rather old. I entered, expecting to see someone barely out of her teens, only to be confronted by white hair and wrinkles. No wonder they'd not been more on guard at her arrival.

Unlike most wannabe Cinderellas, the woman had not worn a ball gown but an ill-fitting hotel uniform. Single shoe sat on the floor by her feet. As mentioned, she held a rather large knife to her throat and stood in the middle of the suite's living room. Killian sat slumped in a chair by the trolley of food with Hannah hovering behind him.

Upon my entry, the old woman's eyes narrowed, and she spat, "Go away, whore. This prince is taken."

I arched a brow. "You can have him. I certainly don't want him."

My reply made her frown. "You're lying."

I waved a hand. "No really, if you want him, he's yours, although I have to say good luck. He's not really a prize what with his overbearing mother, his slovenly attire, and the fact he eats junk food."

Killian gaped in my direction, and Hannah turned from the old woman to hide her smirk.

"You're just saying that to make me go away and steal him for yourself," huffed the old woman.

"Why would I want to marry a prince? I hate having my picture taken. Not keen on following all kinds of stupid rules about royalty, not to mention I like living here in America and have no interest in relocating."

The old lady blinked and, for a second, appeared to be wavering before she shook her head and exclaimed. "Liar, liar, pants on fire."

This would be the point Levi lost his patience. "Listen, lady, I don't want to shoot you, but I will if you don't stop this nonsense right this second. Drop the knife and leave before you force me to do something you won't like."

"Go ahead and kill me," snarled the woman. "I have nothing to lose. My stepkids took everything. I'm living in a room barely fit for vermin. The prince is my ticket to the life I deserve."

"There is help for people in your situation," I stated, moving closer despite Levi's warning grumble.

"I don't want help. I want him!" She aimed her knife at Killian, the moment someone had been waiting for seeing as how a projectile flew past me and hit her in the forehead, stunning her. The water bottle fell to the floor.

The old lady blinked, and her fingers loosened enough the knife fell from her grip. Danger averted.

Or not.

"You'll pay for that," the woman spat as Levi moved in her direction.

It should have been an empty threat, only the old lady began to change, her body rippling unnaturally. Her lips moved soundlessly as she began to grow and grow, her body bulking, tearing the seams of the stolen uniform. Her skin darkened to a slate gray as scales formed.

It took Levi shouting, "Dragon!" for me to understand what I saw.

Holy candy corn. The woman shifted into a giant reptile with wings, big enough the hunch of her back almost touched the ceiling, but more worrisome? Her jaw dropped open, and I could see an orange glow in the back of her throat.

Before I could react, Levi did, dragging me to the floor and covering me with his body as a jet of fire shot past where I'd been standing, hot enough that the exposed parts of me ended up with singed hairs.

Levi rolled from atop me and shouted, "Where's the fucking spear?"

Spear? Oh dear. They were going to kill the woman who never asked for this. There had to be a way to stop the carnage.

At the same time, the dragon was only just beginning her attack.

On me, I should add.

While the dragon lady ignored the prince and his bodyguards, she appeared intent on reaching me. Her neck stretched in my direction, and her teeth clacked. The heat of her breath washed over me, and as I froze in fright, Levi lunged, sword out, stabbing at the chest, only the armored scales deflected the blow. That didn't stop him from hacking at the beast, trying to distract it.

"Cinder, get out of here. And where's the fucking spear?" Levi bellowed.

I would have liked to move, but fear had me planted in place as Hannah hollered, "Gerome's fetching it from his room."

Which would take time and we didn't have any. Already a new batch of flames brewed in the dragon's belly. Steam emerged from her nostrils as she once more opened her maw to spew, with me standing like a statue in her direct line of sight.

A jug of ice water flew right into that opening, startling the dragon, who snapped her jaw shut. A glance showed a cool and composed Killian by the trolley still laden with breakfast.

Despite Levi's barked, "Get out of here, you fool," Killian walked toward the dragon and looked it in the eye.

"I am sorry to disappoint, fair lady. Alas, as you might have surmised, I've already found my bride." He reached out a hand to me without ever taking his gaze from the dragon.

What was he doing? Whatever his plan, his words held the beast's attention, and so I played along, joining him to place my hand in his.

Killian tugged me closer to his side and calmly stated, "The truth is I've already placed a lost shoe on my Cinderella, and it was a perfect fit."

The dragon huffed.

"I know, she shouldn't have lied. She didn't want to injure your obviously large and loving heart."

This time the beast rumbled.

"I fear I am not the prince you've been seeking, but I am sure there is one out there, waiting for you."

The dragon roared, a sound to make any sane person wince. It shook its head, and I felt my hair flutter with the breeze of the shake. I stood close enough that I kept expecting it to chomp me in two.

To everyone's surprise, the dragon whirled around, its whipping tail only missing my ankles because of a fierce yank that dragged me out of the way, along with Killian.

The dragon trundled to the window and, with a smash of glass, threw itself out. For a second, I thought the old woman, now beast, had chosen to kill herself, but a moment later, she rose on extended leathery wings. She flapped off into the bright blue morning sky, a speck that grew smaller and smaller until she was gone.

I whirled on Killian. "I can't believe that worked."

"Me neither," he admitted sheepishly.

Levi, however, didn't seem as impressed. "What kind of foolhardy bullshit was that? You were told to run."

"I am not the type to flee in the face of danger, especially when I'm the cause," he stated.

"Do you know the fucking trouble that would have occurred had that dragon murdered you? And then, to add to your ill judgment, you almost got Cinder killed." Levi shook with rage, and while his fists remained by his side, the tightly clenched fingers showed him barely in control.

I put a hand on his arm. "But everything worked out in the end. We're uninjured, and the old woman wasn't needlessly executed."

Levi turned an icy glare on me. "There's a dragon loose. I wouldn't call that a good thing."

Before I could reply, Gerome returned, long silver spear in hand. "Where did it go?" he exclaimed.

Hannah pointed to the broken window. "It flew away."

"Bummer." The Knight looked utterly dejected.

Killian, however, clapped his hands. "I don't know about you, but I could use some breakfast after that excitement. Since this one is ruined, I say we find that greasy diner and stuff ourselves with bacon and pancakes."

"You can't be serious?" Levi ogled him.

"Well, we can't exactly stay here. The room is a mess, which means we'll need to relocate. The question being, where? I, for one, can't plan on an empty stomach, so what do you say, my fake fiancée?" Killian turned an engaging smile on me. "Shall we dine?" He offered me the crook of his elbow.

Despite Levi's simmering annoyance, I looped my arm through Killian's and chirped, "Lead the way, fair prince."

12

We crowded around a table at the greasy spoon down the street from the hotel. We'd snuck out through the back once more, with the prince wearing a baseball cap and a tie-dyed T-shirt that swirled enough to make anyone staring too long dizzy.

The vinyl-covered booths weren't meant for large men. I got jammed on one side with Levi—thigh to thigh—while Killian sat across with Hannah. Gerome leaned against the counter, while the other Knights roamed around the block, watching for trouble. It hadn't taken much to convince the patrons to leave. Levi's glare sent them scattering, although as each person exited, Hannah mollified them somewhat by handing them hundred-dollar bills for their trouble. The owner had been more than happy to accommodate with the wad of cash thrust her way.

We had the place to ourselves but not a great view since Levi insisted we sit far from the window.

The food emerged quickly and copiously, with Levi tasting everything I loaded onto my plate while Gerome did the same for Killian. Which led to Hannah scowling. "I'm perfectly capable of testing his food." To which Gerome muttered, "Your taste buds can't tell good from bad."

"Are you still going to harp on that damned cake?" Hannah huffed. "It was my first time baking. How was I supposed to know the container with white powdery shit was salt and not sugar?"

"I rest my case." Gerome moved back to the counter after he'd taken a bite of everything and not croaked from poison.

We ate for a bit before Killian broke the sound of chewing to say, "One good thing that emerged from this morning. I think we've found a solution to the Cinderella problem at the upcoming ball."

My fork paused midway to my mouth as Levi asked softly, "How do you figure?"

"The old woman backed down when I declared Cinder as my intended."

"And if she hadn't? Cinder would have been dead." Levi's flat reply.

"But she isn't. It worked." Killian grinned.

"This time." Levi's dour summary.

"It wouldn't be that hard to test it again," Killian declared.

"Meaning what?" Levi gruffly questioned. "You going to parade Cinder in front of the hopefuls mobbing the hotel and see if they all decide to suddenly go home?"

The prince shrugged. "It's a thought."

"And if they all turn into dragons?"

Killian's expression turned thoughtful. "That might be a bit of a problem."

To my surprise, Hannah jumped in to agree with the prince. "He might be onto something. What if we brought in a random wannabe Cinderella and tested in a controlled environment?"

Before Levi could object, I threw my approval into the ring. "I think it's a splendid idea and, honestly, not something I've heard being tried before." Usually, the prince fell under the spell and wanted to find his Cinderella, just like Little Ash couldn't wait to meet her prince. It was only after the wedding the problems usually arose. But in this case, neither of us wanted the other. Could the cure to The Little Ash story be as simple as Killian declaring himself already taken? I wouldn't have thought the curse would be so easily fooled. Then again, the old lady hadn't been cured. She'd exited one curse, only to get caught in the other. What would happen if all those Cinderellas had their storyline changed? Would we have a city full of dragons? Perhaps Levi had a point. At the same time, what if we could help some of these women escape the Grimm Effect?

Levi drummed his fingers on the table. "Guess I'm out voted. If we're going to do this, then it's going to be under strict supervision. The Knights will be armed; guns, tasers, spears. I want to be ready for all possibilities. As well, all Cinderellas-in-waiting will be frisked before entry for weapons. Even if we declare them clear, neither Cinder nor the prince is to touch or come within reach of any of the potentials."

As he ticked off the don'ts, I almost rolled my eyes but held back, mostly because I realized he had a point. We had no idea what to expect or how these women would react. It also occurred to me that his aggressive orders might be because he cared. All of those weeks of us dancing around each other at the bureau and I'd never seen him so focused and grim. I mean, yes, he took his missions seriously, but this felt next level.

As we packed up to leave—and by pack up I meant ordered coffees and pastries to go because Killian was a bottomless pit—a discordant melody made me glance out the window. I blinked at the sight of a cat, upright on its hind legs, walking down the sidewalk, holding a banjo, which it played badly, while yowling.

Lucky me with my affinity for animals, I could understand the rhyme, although it differed from the original.

A cat came strumming out of the alley,
With a banjo in his hands.
He could sing nothing but "Grim-de-dee,
The prince will marry his Ashy lady.
Growl, Sir Knight.
Cry, jilted lover!
For a wedding there will be at the ball.

Killian snorted. "Next thing you know, pigs will be flying and we'll see cows jumping over the moon."

"I'd think you'd be more worried with your appetite that the dish might run away with the spoon before you're done eating," Hannah teased.

As for Levi, he muttered, "The world has gone mad."

It had, but at least we'd found each other.

For now.

Look at me, my thoughts now sounding as ominous as my future lover.

13

Since no one mentioned it, I assumed my companions had not heard the cat's odd rhyme. Probably a good thing seeing as how the verse claimed there would be a marriage at the ball. For some reason, remembering it left me chilled to the bone. I didn't want to assume it referred to me, and yet, the word knight could only refer to Levi. Who else would be growling and upset?

This had to be the Grimm Effect doing its best to throw me off balance, to push for the conclusion it wanted. Never mind the fact neither Killian nor I wanted to get married. Not to each other at least.

I might have dwelled on it more, but the afternoon proved busy. For one, we relocated the prince to the same floor as the Knights—Gerome gave up his room for the prince. Smaller and less luxurious but Killian preferred to remain in the hotel because, as he claimed, the ball was only two days away and he should be nearby in case management needed him to make any last-minute changes or decisions.

By late afternoon, the prince had held some meetings with government officials as part of the treaty talks that involved a trade deal that would see Corsica increasing its exports of wine and their specialty honey, plus waiving the need for visas for tourists. In return, the USA would be lowering the tariffs on the goods as well as setting up an embassy.

It should be noted I wasn't part of those talks. I worked in a conference room that held a minimum of two Knights at all times. Levi's orders. He kept popping in and out as I worked out the details of our upcoming test trial with the Cinderellas. Hannah had been observing the crowd and pulling some of the—and I quote—"Non-crazy-eyed hopefuls."

Those selected were brought to the hotel bar and provided Hannah with their identification as well as answered some basic questions.

Why are you here? *To marry the prince.*

Do you have any weapons on you? *Just my killer smile/body/personality.*

Mind giving a sample of your blood? *Sure.*

Any answers that strayed from the above got sent back out to join those crowding the barricades.

To those who might wonder at the blood request, we wanted a baseline sample should any of them happen to shift into another dragon or something worse. The scientists would want to compare the before and after to see if they spotted any identifying markers.

All in all, a busy day and it wasn't yet done. We had dinner before our experiment with the Ash-hopefuls. A dinner that left an already grim Levi looking practically carved in stone by the end of it. He might have helped with the planning, but he still didn't like it.

The conference room we'd prepared had nothing that could be used as a weapon. However, it did have a window, unlike some of the inner chambers in the hotel. Levi had wanted a contained room, but Killian had argued, "If we get another dragon, I'd rather see it fly free than end up dead from our experiment."

The prince won, and so we sat on one side of the room, at the head of the long table, flanked by Levi and Hannah, while potentials were brought in one by one.

The first to entered was Cindy-mae, a lovely umber-skinned woman with the most gorgeous eyes and shapely figure showcased by her pale yellow mermaid gown.

She entered with her head held high until she saw me. Then, like the old woman, her lip curled. "Begone, foul stepsister. Thou doth not belong here." Cindy-mae had truly embraced the old fairytale, language and all.

Rather than reply, I let Killian take the lead.

"Hi." He didn't believe in formal address unless totally necessary. He'd even changed from his princely attire he'd worn all afternoon for the government officials to his casual clothes for these meetings. "Nice to meet you."

The deep curtsy that Cindy-mae dropped into left me in awe. I probably would have collapsed if I tried one like it.

"Your Majesty," she murmured. "I am honored you chose to meet me before the ball."

"About that... Why are you here, Cindy-mae?" he asked bluntly.

"Why to marry you, of course," Cindy-mae declared without hesitation.

"Why me? We've never met before now."

"Because we're destined to be together forever. For I am the one you have been seeking, and we shall live happily ever after," Cindy-mae sang, swaying in place.

And this was what Hannah called not so crazy?

"Alas, I'm afraid that's not possible. You see, I've

already chosen my bride-to-be." Killian turned to me with a smile. "I've found my true love, and we shall be wed at the ball."

"You would choose my wicked stepsister over me?" Cindy-mae huffed. "But she doesn't even fit in the shoe." The woman bent down to pluck an impressively high stiletto and waved it. The glass caught the light.

"Why would she fit in your shoe when she has her own?" Killian plopped a golden slipper on the table, one bought from a nearby store in my size. "Darling, if you would?"

"Of course, sweetie." We'd decided earlier to play the part of lovey-dovey couple. I placed my bare foot on the table, and he slid the shoe on.

"A perfect fit," Killian declared.

Cindy-mae gaped. "But... I don't understand. The ball hasn't happened yet. How could you have her shoe?"

My turn. "We met at a discotheque last night. After a night of dancing, I lost it getting into a cab, and the prince was kind of enough to track me down to return it." I smiled vapidly in his direction.

"You're really going to marry *her?*" Cindy-mae's lip curled.

"I am. Sorry." Killian even sounded apologetic. "You'll have to find another prince worthy of you."

I could see the woman visibly shudder then stiffen. "In that case, I don't want to waste your time. I see this was a mistake. If you'll excuse me." Cindy-mae swept out, shoe in hand, clomping unevenly, but best of all, she remained human.

When the door shut, Killian sighed. "That went better than expected."

Unfortunately, not all of the meetings with candidates picked for the experiment went so smoothly.

Despite patting all the Cinderella-hopefuls down, some managed to create weapons.

There was Gertrude with lavishly coiffed hair who leaped onto the table and ran for me, pulling out a long pin from her tresses before having her ankles swept by Hannah.

Chubby-cheeked and twinkling-eyed Jolene threw her shoe, which spun and missed my head, only because Levi yanked me out of its path. The heel planted into the wall a few inches deep. Jolene got escorted out, noisily sobbing.

Luckily, none of the jilted potentials turned into dragons, although we did get one frog, who hopped away croaking, and a swan who hissed in our direction before heading for the window, which Hannah quickly opened so she might fly free. We even met one woman who suddenly flipped into a witch and did some damage. Miss Juliette McIntyre went from a meek and sweet-looking young woman with a guileless expression to suddenly wearing a dark form-fitting gown and flinging lightning bolts. Gerome tasered Juliette and carted her out for processing by the bureau. We took a hard line on violent magic users.

Through it all, I played my part. Smiling, batting my lashes at Killian, getting a shoe placed on my foot over and over.

At ten o'clock, Killian yawned. "I think that's enough for one day."

"Not bad, you broke the hearts of twenty-three women," Hannah noted looking up from the tablet where she'd been keeping track.

"Leaving how many?" he asked.

"Two hundred and three. We had more suddenly appear on the guest list late afternoon."

Killian groaned. "We'll never disappoint them all in time."

"No, but the important part is we know what seems to work," I pointed out to lift his spirits.

"Is it working though?" Killian asked, his expression serious. "Or will the curse keep sending me Cinderellas until I finally cave?"

"Maybe you'll meet one you like and actually marry her, putting a stop to it." I tried to offer him hope.

"I would like nothing more. However, in the meantime, I'll keep having to deal with this."

Hannah offered a sly solution. "You know, there is such a thing as a marriage of convenience. You could always just fake it. Find someone who doesn't mind being a trophy wife, at least until you meet the one."

"Who would agree?" he asked at large. A question no one had a reply to.

Levi appeared to be in a foul mood as we returned to our room. I could have pried, but my menagerie cheered upon my entry so I spent some time on the floor letting them climb over me, replying to their chittering, while rubbing Izzy's spine.

Eventually, I had to deal with the grumpy Knight who stood staring out the window.

"Care to explain your foul mood?" I asked.

"How much of what I saw downstairs was an act?"

Don't tell me I had a jealous Knight on my hands. On that point, I could easily reassure. "All of it was a fake."

He whirled. "Are you sure? Because it looked and sounded convincing."

"Of course, it did." I rolled my eyes. "What did you expect? We had to make these women believe Killian wasn't available. Can't exactly do that if we're scowling at each other."

"I'd understand if you wanted to marry him. He

would be a good match for you." Spoken stiffly through a rigid jaw.

"According to who? Because it certainly isn't me. I find myself rather attracted to an ornery warrior who has yet to give me a kiss, even though we're finally alone."

He didn't need any more invitation than that. He plucked me from the floor and held me aloft as he devoured my mouth, leaving me breathless.

"About time," I murmured.

"Trust me when I say I wanted to be alone with you hours ago."

"Oh really? Prove it," my impish reply, to which he groaned.

His arms wrapped even tighter, keeping me pinned against his body. He started out coaxing, parting my lips to tease me with his tongue. I moaned as pleasure suffused me. I'd been kissed before but nothing like this. In the past, a kiss was just that. With Levi, it was like being tossed into a storm. A wildness filled me. Arousal simmered. Need demanded.

And he provided.

He nibbled my lips, and I teased his right back. My arms linked around his neck while my legs wrapped around his waist, holding me against his erection. His hands cupped my bottom, and he ground me against him, giving me pressure where I most wanted it.

When his lips nuzzled my neck, I tilted my head back and enjoyed the feel of his mouth dragging down my tender flesh. I leaned back so he could move lower, and with one hand, he palmed my back, urging me to arch my chest while his other hand teased the tops of my breast—a tease with too much fabric in the way.

"Undress me." I uttered the soft command, and he groaned.

"As my princess commands."

He set me down but only so he could remove my clothing. Shirt. Pants. He took a moment to stare at me standing there in my bra and panties.

He sighed. "You're much too beautiful."

In his eyes I certainly felt it. I didn't worry if my breasts were too small, my hips too narrow. His expression smoldered as he took me in.

"Your turn."

"I wasn't done."

"In a second…" I murmured as I let my hands skim his torso, tugging free the shirt that covered that wide and deliciously muscled chest.

I made quick work of his belt buckle, but when I undid the button to his pants, he placed a hand over mine. "Let me."

I sat down to watch as he undid the zipper and shoved them down his legs. His black briefs could barely contain his shaft.

Oh my. I'd never had one this big. I licked my lips, and he groaned.

"If you don't stop being so sexy, I'll never make it."

My lips quirked. "If that happens, I'm sure you'll find another way to satisfy me."

Wait, did I actually say that out loud? Judging by his growl as he stepped for me, I had. My bra hit the floor, as did my panties, leaving me just as nude as him.

But did he toss me to the bed to ravage? Nope. He once more chose to stare, the hunger in him clear to see.

It gave me the boldness to cup my breasts and present them in offering.

"Oh hell yes." He knelt to rub his face between them while I dug my fingers into his hair.

I didn't need to tell him what I wanted. He just knew, sucking my nipple, nipping it before taking as much of my breast as he could into his mouth. His arm wrapped around my waist and dragged me close to him, lifting me off the ground so he could march me to the closest wall. He pressed me up against it, his body acting as an anchor, while he proceeded to tease my breasts. Drawing my aching peaks into his mouth, his tongue swirling over my nipples. Each time he tugged a tip with his lips and teeth, I felt it between my legs. Felt my desire growing stronger and stronger.

As he played, I ground myself against him, my

pussy pressed against his hard belly, soaking it with my arousal. What a waste. I squirmed, trying to get what I wanted.

What I needed.

Again, he understood, and he returned to kissing me while one of his hands grabbed his shaft. He held his body slightly apart and rubbed the head of it against my clit.

My breath hiccupped.

"Are you sure you want this?" he murmured against my mouth.

"Am I not wet enough for you?" I retorted.

He chuckled. "Is that an invitation to taste?"

Oh. I shuddered. I would love to have his mouth on me, but I doubted I'd last more than a few seconds. Besides, I really wanted something else. Something hard. Long. Thick.

"Not this time. I want you inside me."

His turn to tremble. "I don't have a condom."

"I'm on birth control. Please, Levi. I don't think I can wait any longer." I'd never felt so wild and needy. As if I might just die if he didn't fill me up.

He teased me some more, dragging the head of his shaft over my slit. Rubbing against my clit. Making me moan.

I grabbed his hair and kissed him hard, my mouth mashing against his. When his lips parted, my tongue slipped into play, sliding along his, drawing forth a rumble.

"You're going to make me lose control again," he groaned.

"Good." Said with emphatic satisfaction.

With a growl of surrender, he gave me what I wanted. Slowly, though. His cock easing into me, stretching me. It took forever for him to sink to the hilt. A torturous pleasure that had me digging my nails into him and clenching tight.

"Fuck me, princess. You're going to kill me."

"Not before you make me come," I whispered against his lips.

His hands went to gripping my ass, holding those cheeks tight as he began to move inside me. Slow, short thrusts that had me clenching. In and out, we found a rhythm where he bounced me, pushing deep, giving me the friction I desired.

It didn't take much to make me climax. I yelled as I came, my whole body tightening, squeezing him tight. And he followed in that same moment, his cock thrusting deep and holding as it pulsed, spilling within but remaining hard.

Still connected, he carried me to the bed. To my shock, he kept going, thrusting in and out until my pleasure built again.

The second orgasm left me limp and so satisfied I practically purred.

He murmured, "My sweet princess. What did I do to deserve you?"

"Nothing," I whispered back. "I'm the lucky one."

I'd finally found love.

14

When the mice ran up our bodies, using us as their path to the clock, I ignored them because, sure enough, when the clock struck one, they ran down. However, I didn't go immediately back to sleep because a sexy Knight decided to hickory dickory my dock, and I can't say that I minded. Actually, I came really hard.

Our morning nookie happened in the shower, and we'd just finished when Hannah knocked. Given our sopping-wet heads and dewy skin, there was no hiding what happened. Then again, the great big hickey on my neck kind of gave it away.

A much more relaxed Levi dropped a kiss on my lips and a murmured, "I'll be back soon as I can," before he left me in Hannah's care.

"So, you and the boss, eh?" she drawled with a smirk.

I wrinkled my nose. "You don't approve?"

"Oh, I approve. That man needed to get laid, and quite honestly, you're better than the usual one-night-stand skanks he goes for."

My mouth rounded. "That's not nice."

"Actually, it's a compliment," she added. "You're the first woman I've ever seen him spend the night with. Also, the first one he's ever kept around afterwards."

"For now," I murmured. "After all, he has no choice but to be close to me because of the job he was assigned."

Hannah snorted. "Levi is choosing to be near you. Otherwise, you'd be in a different room."

"He thinks I'm in danger."

"If that were true, then he would have us bunking together. I have two beds, too," Hannah stated.

He'd lied? "What? He told me you only had a single."

For some reason, my reply had her guffawing. "I didn't think the boss had it in him to be sly to get a woman alone. About time someone tied him in knots."

"You think he likes me?" I mean I should think he did; after all, we'd become lovers. However, I couldn't forget my initial qualms about him. About how our differences made us an impossible match. Then again, they did say opposites attract.

"He more than likes you, honey. The man is utterly besotted."

A thought that warmed me through and through.

"What's on the agenda today?" Hannah asked.

"Killian's got some meetings this morning, but we thought we'd try and get rid of a few more potentials before the ball tomorrow."

"I don't know that there's any point. The list grew again overnight."

"More Cinderellas?" I ogled her. The number already gathered proved unprecedented.

"Yeah, they're pouring out of the woodwork."

I rubbed my forehead. "The ball is going to be a nightmare."

"I'm thinking more like the aftermath will be. They're all going to be dropping shoes in front of Killian. And if he doesn't choose one, who knows what will happen? We're going to have to be on high alert for assassination from disgruntled potentials. I also wouldn't rule out a kidnapping, but most likely, we'll have a riot."

I'd not actually thought that far ahead. Would things get ugly if he didn't select a bride? "Poor Killian."

"It might be possible to avert disaster. I'm thinking maybe the ball would be the perfect place for you to announce a fake engagement. Hit them all at once."

"That seems dangerous. You saw what happened yesterday with that woman who suddenly turned witch."

"That kind of shit might still happen if the prince leaves that ball without being engaged."

My lips turned down. "I hate this curse."

"We all do, honey."

I eyed her. "Think Levi would go for it?"

"Nope." Hannah shook her head. "I think he will rant and rave and bluster."

"Because it's a dangerous idea."

"More like he'll be insanely jealous. I've never seen a man so tense. Every time you cooed at Killian I thought he'd crush his own hand he fisted it so tight."

"Let me think about it." While I found myself basking in Levi's possessiveness, I wanted to help Killian. At the same time, I couldn't ignore how it bothered Levi when I pretended affection for another.

"You have until the ball to figure it out. In the meantime, I'm bored, and since we can't go outside, I say we hit the pool for a swim."

"Levi will throw a hissy fit if I leave this room."

"His orders were to not leave the hotel and to stick

close to me. He didn't actually say it had to be in this particular spot," Hannah cajoled, finding a loophole.

A swim would be nice. "I don't have a suit."

"I have a spare. It might be a little big, but it will just be the two of us. Gerome will make sure of that."

I couldn't resist a change of scenery and pace. In short order, I wore the one-piece swimsuit borrowed from Hannah, which hung a tad loose. As promised, the pool area, smelling heavily of chlorine, had been cleared and Gerome stood watch.

"Last one in has to marry the prince," Hannah chirped, diving right in.

I took more time, dipping a toe in the shallow end, the water not exactly warm. I submersed my feet first then slowly walked down the steps until the water hit my hips.

While Hannah splashed and flipped, playing like a dolphin, I chose to do a more sedate front stroke. Arms moving in a slow windmill. Feet fluttering. Face in water, sideways to breathe.

With each lap, I felt my tension easing. Only another day and a half to go. Once the ball ended, the prince would head back to his country, I'd return to my desk at the bureau, and Levi... I didn't know what would happen with him.

Would we still see each other?

Date?

Or would he see it as his chance to move on to his next conquest?

Something brushed by my foot. I glanced down, expecting to see Hannah, only the suddenly murky water didn't show anything.

"What's up with the water?" I asked as I began to move toward Hannah, who stood on the pool deck, toweling off.

Oddly, she didn't reply.

I began to stroke for the side when, once more, something passed by my leg. Most likely another fish. I hoped. I tried to not think about the rhyme featuring a crocodile.

My fingers clasped the edge of the pool, and I pulled to haul myself out. My upper body and hips cleared the water, but before I could fully emerge, a yank on my ankle pulled me under!

I flailed and kicked, trying to reach for the surface, but whatever had a firm grip on my leg didn't relent.

Despite the pool only being about fifteen feet at its deepest part, I sank farther. Far enough my lungs began to strain and spots danced behind my closed lids.

Whatever held me wasn't letting go, and as darkness grabbed me tight, I heard a voice whisper, *Are you worthy?*

15

I REGAINED CONSCIOUSNESS—SHIVERING, wet, cold, scared—inside a damp cave lit in a yellow and green glow that appeared to emanate from the walls. It came from some kind of moss that I'd never seen before, unfamiliar, like the place I found myself.

Where am I? Last thing I remembered I was sinking in the hotel pool because something dragged me under. At least I hadn't drowned. At the same time, my current situation appeared bleak. Sorry, but I couldn't recall a single story where waking up in a cave boded well.

I rose and wrapped my arms around my upper body as if that would stop the shaking. It didn't. The damp swimsuit clung to my clammy body, and I didn't see anything to dry or wrap myself in.

The cave had a high ceiling, at least eight or nine feet, and spanned just as wide. The only thing other than me? Bones. All kinds of bones. Some the thin skeletons of fish, but the human skull? That had me gulping.

The stone cavern had a single opening, and I hesitated before poking my head out, a quick peek, where I readied to duck back in case something took a swipe. In that brief glimpse, I saw another cave, a much larger one, lit by the same glowing moss but also gelatinous bulbs that pulsed on the walls and on the ceiling that arched high overhead. Seeing no signs of danger, I stepped into the larger space, which held a pool of water, ringed by pale stone, the surface of it smooth, unlike the walls. Water dripped from overhead, the occasional droplets disturbing the still surface of a small, clear blue lake.

I chose to walk the perimeter of the place, looking for any kind of clue as to my location or captor. I also kept an eye out for a way to escape. It took me doing an entire circuit before I realized there didn't appear to be any exit. No holes large enough for me to squeeze through. No cracks I could slip in sideways. Nothing to indicate how I'd even arrived, which led my gaze to the lake. Whatever kidnapped me must have dragged me via an underwater tunnel and trapped me here. But why?

Food, most likely. I couldn't forget the bones in the other room. It spurred my urgency to leave before whatever lived here chose to return. Could I escape via the lake? I knelt by its edge and stared into the clear water. I could see the channel dropped straight down, so far I couldn't see any signs of a tunnel. Deep enough that I wouldn't stand a chance with a single breath, not with my only adequate swimming skills.

I plopped my butt on the hard stone and sighed. "Fairy godmother, if you can hear me, now might be a good time for you to grant me a wish."

Nothing stirred the air; however, the water did ripple. Ominous, hence why I scuttled away until my back hit the wall.

A head emerged from the lake first, the hair long and dark green, framing a face of a paler shade. A woman rose from the water, beautiful if not quite human, with smooth features, a flattened nose, lips full and dark, with eyes of pure black. Despite never having met one, I recognized what I faced.

A Nixie!

She leaned her forearms on the edge of the lake and cocked her head. "You are smaller than I would have expected. Older too. Not many prime childbearing years left on you and terrible hips."

My mouth rounded. "Excuse me?"

"No, you are not excused. You are not what I would have chosen at all."

Rather than focus on her comments thus far, I blurted out, "Who are you? Why did you abduct me?"

"I am Nicola, and I took you because I wanted to meet the female who stole my son."

I blinked. "I'm sorry. I don't understand. I haven't stolen anyone."

"Don't lie. His scent is all over you." Her lip curled.

She could only mean Levi, and if she recognized the smell of him, then she could only be... "You're the Nixie who kept him prisoner!"

"He lived with me, yes." Her lips pursed. "And now he does not. It's been a while since he's visited."

"Why would he visit his captor?"

"Hardly his captor. His father gave him over freely."

"But you wouldn't let him go."

She shrugged. "Those were the terms set out. It is not in my power to break them."

"I've made no bargain with you. Why have you taken me?"

"Because I want to know if you're worthy of my son."

"Isn't that up to Levi?" I blurted out.

"I guess we will see how much value he places in

you shortly. He'll know by now that you're gone. Do you think he will care?"

I wanted to scream yes, but at the same time, I couldn't be sure. He was a cold-blooded killer. A man who showed little to no remorse when he had to do bad things. Would he dare confront the Nixie who'd kept him captive for me? Or would he fear she'd take him prisoner again? She kept calling him son, meaning she thought she had some sort of claim.

"How's Levi supposed to even know I'm here with you?" I countered. "Not to mention, how is it any of your business if he cares for me or not?"

"Because he is the son I couldn't have, the child I raised, and while he might have fled the waters to forge his own path, I watch over him still. I will always protect him. Especially from the unworthy." Her lips pursed as she eyed me and left me feeling wanting.

"You can't keep me here." A faint claim with little fire.

"Who says I am? You may leave anytime you want." She pointed to the water at her back. "But I should warn that outside this cavern there are dangers. Things that would love to eat wiggling little toes. That would feed on tender flesh. Even if you were to survive their teeth, it is a long swim to shore."

"How long?"

Her lips curved into a cold smile. "Let's just say you only made it because of my magic."

Meaning I'd drown before I ever even made it close. As the reality of Nicola's words penetrated, the true horror sank in. I'd gone from being a Cinderella avoiding marriage to a prince to a prisoner with no hope of escape because no way would Levi risk his freedom for me.

So much for the brief happiness I found.

"WHAT DO YOU MEAN SHE DISAPPEARED?" Levi bellowed as he stood by the edge of the pool. The clear water showed no body at the bottom. Worrisome to the extreme since he didn't see Cinder anywhere in the vicinity, despite there being only one exit and Gerome swore on his life she'd not emerged.

Hannah wrung her hands in a rare sign of anxiety. "It's like I said. One minute we were swimming, and the next, she was gone. Like poof gone." She exploded her hands.

"That makes no sense," he growled. "What the fuck possessed you to take her swimming?"

"I thought she needed a change of scenery. It should have been safe. I was with her the entire time. Gerome made sure no one else entered."

It made him think of the fish in the tub the other night. A fish that had suddenly appeared. Had the same thing happened here? Had something apparated in the water and taken Cinder?

The very thought boiled his rage rather than his fear because he refused to give in to that kind of despair. She had to be alive.

And I will find her.

"I'm going in the water," he stated, stripping his shirt.

"To do what? There's nothing there," Hannah insisted, waving her hand at the pool. He could have counted the tiles the water shone so clear.

"Maybe what we see is an illusion." The Grimm Effect could play tricks on the mind.

"What if it takes you too?" Hannah showed a rare worry.

"Then at least I'll know what happened to Cinder." His sweet princess. He'd been hard-pressed to leave her that morning. The feelings inundating his entire being had taken him by storm. They began the first moment they met, weeks ago. He'd seen her slight figure hunched over a keyboard as she worked diligently, chewing her bottom lip adorably, looking intense with concentration. His attraction had only grown. Not just because of her looks but her intelligence. She'd been more than useful on his recent missions, gathering intel that he'd have thought impossible. Guiding them in the right direction. But what cemented it? The way she stood up to him—him and no one else. While she did her job competently and firmly, she tended to be easygoing with everyone except him. Unlike so many, she didn't fear him. He didn't intimidate her.

It only made him want her more.

He'd fought his interest in her, had to because she deserved better than a damaged Knight. But this latest task that put them in close proximity... It had been too much for him to resist. How could he say no when she kissed him? How could he walk away when she brought him such pleasure?

How could she be gone?

The air suddenly sizzled unnaturally. Even as he yelled, "Incoming," he drew his gun, ready to shoot.

A woman appeared, the type you might call ageless with her fairly smooth skin yet so thin it could have been parchment, her hair gray and white. The lady, whom he'd met before, wore a poufy gown of pastel yellow that he rated almost as ridiculous as the tiny tiara that matched the wand she held. Weirder than Agatha suddenly appearing, the fact she appeared to float above the pool deck.

"What do you want? Where's Cinder?" Because

surely someone who could appear and disappear at will had something to do with his missing princess.

"Hello to you too, Sir Knight."

Hannah chirped, "Holy shit, it's Cinder's godmother."

"I'm aware who it is," he growled. "And I'm asking again, where is Cinder?"

"I'm afraid that's a tad complicated." Godmother sank to the floor, her lips downturned. "It's also why I'm here. I am sorry to inform you that Cinder is gone."

"She's dead?" Hannah gasped.

"Oh dearie no. She's alive," Agatha quickly corrected, offering him some relief.

"Where has Cinder gone?" he asked.

"Not somewhere you can easily fetch her I fear."

"Listen, lady, would you stop talking in circles and answer the fucking question." Levi lost patience as they wasted time dancing around the subject.

"Goodness, you lack manners. It's kind of refreshing. I'm so used to people either fawning over me or making ridiculous wishes that it's kind of nice." Godmother beamed.

"My manners are going to get worse if you don't start talking," he growled.

"In that case, let me get to the point. It appears

Cinder has been taken by a Nixie. The same one you escaped so long ago."

He blinked as he digested this bit of information. Then exploded. "What the fuck do you mean Nicola took her?"

"I'm afraid I'm not clear on the details. Simply that the Nixie somehow managed to create a gateway to this pool, allowing her to kidnap Cinder and take her back to her lair."

"Fuck me, that isn't good." Levi recalled all too well the games Nicola used to make him play. Forcing him to hold his breath underwater to strengthen his lungs. Withholding nourishment, thus forcing him to scrounge, which, in turn, made him self-sufficient. Tossing him into the waters to fight sharks and eels, which contributed to his strength. Cinder would never survive!

"Agreed, but I don't know what we can do. The Nixie is beyond my ability to reach." Agatha apologized.

"But not out of mine," he muttered. Levi stripped off his shirt and kicked off his boots.

Hannah huffed, "What do you think you're doing?"

"Fetching Cinder, of course." It should have been obvious.

"In case you hadn't noticed, that's a pool. Not the home for a Nixie."

"It's a body of water, meaning I can find the path there."

"Are you serious?" Hannah ogled him.

"Have ever known me not to be?"

Hannah waved her hands. "But you can't leave. We're a day away from the ball. The prince—"

"Has other Knights to watch over him. I shouldn't be more than a few hours."

"Hours?" Hannah screeched. "What if we get another dragon?"

"Gerome can spear it."

"What if the prince is kidnapped?"

"Then you'll have some explaining to do," his dark reply.

Hannah's lips pursed. "You really think it's wise to leave now to find Cinder?"

"Yes. And don't even think of stopping me."

"Why would I stop a man in love?" Hannah chuckled.

The L word tensed him head to toe. "I am not in love."

Hannah smirked. "Sure you aren't, says Mr. Responsibility, who is ditching the mission to go after a woman."

"Cinder is more than just a woman."

"Apparently," Hannah murmured slyly.

"Wait, did I miss something since my last visit?" Agatha asked as she eyed them, trying to keep up.

"Your last visit?" Hannah asked curiously.

"I don't have time for this. You're in charge until my return." With that, Levi dove into the water and closed his eyes as he stroked for the bottom of the pool. The nerve of Nicola, abducting Cinder.

Unacceptable.

Stroke. Stroke. His arms pulled, his legs kicked, and when he didn't hit the bottom, he knew he'd found the watery path to the Nixie's lair. Now the true danger began. A good thing his old lessons were firmly entrenched and his lungs still strong from the conditioning.

By the time he heaved himself from the pool of water into the cave where he'd been raised, he'd fought a great white—and only gotten scrapes across his knuckles—tied an octopus in knots—and ignored the urge to have it deep fried—and been jolted by an electric eel. To say his mood was foul would be putting it mildly. He bellowed as he emerged, "Nicola! What did you do with my princess?"

The Nixie sat at a rusty bistro table, her hair a curtain over her nude body, her smile wide as she greeted him. "Hello, son. How nice of you to visit."

"This isn't a social call." His gaze hit Cinder next,

looking bedraggled but otherwise safe sitting across from Nicola wearing a seaweed cape.

His heart stopped when she smiled at him and said, "I can't believe you came."

Fuck me. Hannah had pegged it.

He was in fucking love.

16

I blinked in astonishment when Levi appeared, emerging from the water like an angry sea god wearing only black briefs and a glower. Oh my. Bad timing, but I'd never been so turned on. To those who might question my sanity, given my situation and initial trepidation, I'd relaxed somewhat as the Nixie proved herself to not be a murderous water sprite. It helped she'd not tried to kill me. On the contrary, she'd turned into an attentive hostess who had some giant crabs set up a table and chairs for us as well as a meal. While I wouldn't usually be the type to eat raw fish, the sushi she offered proved tasty.

However, I forgot about the food in my pleasure at seeing my dark Knight. He'd come for me!

"Of course, I came. Are you injured?" he demanded.

I shook my head. "I was a tad chilly upon my arrival, but Nicola was kind enough to provide me with a mantle to cut the cold." Woven of seaweed, she'd drawn the moisture from it. Once I wrapped it around my shoulders, it did much to reduce my shivering.

"Did you just call her kind?" He bit out the word. "She shouldn't have taken you in the first place." His glare should have incinerated the Nixie on the spot.

"I had every right to want to meet the woman who captured your interest. *Son.*"

The appellation still startled because I knew she wasn't his mother, and yet Levi didn't correct her. "Have you completely forgotten our discussion about not meddling in my life?"

"Maybe I wouldn't have to if someone kept in touch," Nicola riposted.

"I've been busy."

"Too busy to visit. Too busy to hop into a pond or a lake to send me a message." Nicola sniffed. "Children today are so ungrateful."

Levi raked his fingers through his damp hair as he gritted through a tight jaw, "We spoke just last week."

"Briefly and I don't recall a mention of your lady friend." Nicola waved a delicate hand in my direction.

"Because there was nothing to tell."

"Ha. Lying to your mother. Did you think I wouldn't notice your mark on her?"

"What are you talking about?" he growled.

"The moment she hit the water, I sensed your claim, and so I decided to meet the woman who'd ensnared my son."

Wait, what claim? The conversation implied things that had me curious.

"You kidnapped her!" he barked.

"I wouldn't call it kidnapping, more like extending an invitation she couldn't refuse," Nicola declared.

"You had no right."

"I had every right." Nicola didn't raise her voice, and yet her words held an icy edge. "You are my son. The babe I raised. Cared for. Loved. And now you are entangled with a woman whom I've never met. A woman who is meant for another."

I felt a need to interject. "If you're talking about the Little Ash curse, then I'd like to say I have no intention of marrying the prince."

"As if you have a choice." Nicola waved a hand. "We are all part of a story, playing our roles to their conclusions. And yours doesn't include my son. As Levi's mother, it is up to me to protect him."

"I don't need your protection," he grumbled.

"You can't make me stop caring," Nicola huffed.

"Care all you want but leave Cinder out of it. You

will release her at once." He crossed his arms and offered his most fierce expression.

"I will release Cinder but on one condition." Nicola tilted her head to face me. "She must swear to never break your heart."

"Mother..." Levi injected a warning tone.

"Don't you mother me." Nicola's sharp retort held a firm edge. "You deserve happiness, and I will not let anyone, especially not this slip of a girl, hurt you in any way."

"I can handle disappointment," he drawled.

"I'd rather you didn't have to."

Seeing them argue, I had a simple solution. "I agree to your terms."

"No, you don't. This is an unreasonable request." Levi's head swiveled as he frowned in my direction.

"Not really because I have no intention of hurting you."

"Who says you could?" his harsh reply.

Nicola's head bobbed between us. "Perhaps I was mistaken. I was under the impression you cared for the girl."

"It's just sex," I exclaimed, only to blush. "I would never presume to think Levi felt anything more." Even if I did.

"Just sex?" For some reason, his glower returned stronger than before.

"I'm aware I'm not your usual type and that we're complete opposites. I mean you're fearless and strong, while I'm not. You probably want a partner in life who's a warrior like you. Who squishes the spiders instead of befriending them. I am fully aware that what we have now, while immensely pleasurable, most likely won't last." My lips turned down. "If anyone's heart will be broken, it's mine."

I thought his eyes would pop out of his head. "You think I'll ditch you?"

"You don't have to pretend. Hannah said you're not the type to want a relationship."

"Hannah can suck it. She doesn't know how I feel or what I want."

"What do you want?" I asked, point blank.

"You." A simple word and my heart almost burst.

"But we're so different." I couldn't have said why I felt a need to argue.

"And?"

I couldn't help but smile as I rose from the chair and took a step in his direction. "Do you really think we could make it work?"

"I'm not afraid to try."

"This might be the one time in my life where I can find the courage to forge into the unknown." Because I had a strong feeling loving Levi would be worth it.

He closed the distance between us and clasped my

hands. "This will be a journey we take together, without interference or threats." The last he directed at Nicola.

His adoptive/kidnapping mother smiled. "Well, this has been enlightening. In light of the facts, Cinder is free to go."

"Without restriction," Levi commanded. "I won't have her coerced into feeling things for me that aren't real."

"Yes, yes." Nicola waved her hand. "If this is what you wish, then I guess I can only give my blessing. Although, if you do hurt my son"—her voice lowered—"there won't be a lake or a pond or even a bathtub that will hide you from my wrath."

"Mother!" His tone held warning, but I grinned.

"I promise to do my best to make him happy for as long as he'll have me."

"Be careful what you vow, princess. What if I want forever?" his low rumbled murmur.

I glanced at him and meant it when I said, "It might just be long enough."

His fierce kiss stole my breath and tingled me head to toe and was sadly interrupted by his pseudo-mother clapping.

"I cannot wait to meet my grandbabies," Nicola exclaimed.

Babies?

Poor Levi looked just as shocked by the idea.

"Let's not get ahead of ourselves," he stammered.

To save him, I reminded him of his duty. "We really should get back to Prince Killian."

"Yes, we should." He stiffened, and the warrior expression returned. "Seeing as how I can't give Cinder breath for the lengthy route you always make me take, we'll need a shortcut she can survive."

"In return for what?" Nicola asked with a sly look.

When it appeared as if Levi would explode, I extended an offer. "I shall name my firstborn daughter Nicola. And if a son, Nicholas."

"Done!" The Nixie beamed and, at the same time, surged, her body morphing into a wave that pushed us into the lake.

I might have yelled but for the water. I held my breath as I clung tight to Levi, my solid rock in the undertow that carried us down that deep well. The cold chilled me to the bone, but Levi's grip offered warmth and reassurance.

When the current abated and my head popped out of the water, I parted my lips for a deep breath before I opened my eyes to see us bobbing in the pool.

Back at the hotel. Alive. Uninjured. Together... But was Levi happy? Not according to his expression.

"We made it," I chirped.

"Mmph." His grunt as he stroked to the edge of the pool and hoisted me out.

I stood and shook like a wet dog before grabbing the towel Hannah left behind. Two of them. One for me and another for Levi.

I dried and cast a glance at my grumpy Knight. "You seem pissed."

"I'm fine." A curt reply.

"Nicola is quite the interesting character."

He snorted. "That's an understatement."

"Does she always kidnap your lovers?"

"This is the first time and the last," he snapped. "I don't know what she was thinking."

"She cares." An odd thing to say given the situation. When I'd originally heard the abbreviated story of him being given to the Nixie, I'd assumed the worst. I mean he was given over as a baby without a care by his father. His biological mother died in childbirth. I expected to hear of a childhood of abuse. Yet it seemed instead she'd nurtured and, in doing so, became a mother that Levi still kept in contact with.

"She was meddling," he grumbled.

"You should be glad she is concerned about your well-being," I huffed to her defense. "I would have given anything growing up for someone to give a hoot about me. It was always 'Cinder, clean this.' 'Cinder, go away.' I slept in the basement by the cat litter. Got leftovers for my meals. My clothing, the worst of the hand-me-downs, and I only got those because child services stepped in after the school lodged a complaint about my ill-fitting rags."

He paused in his drying to stare at me. "They abused you."

I shrugged. "They did. Not really a surprise, as it's part of the Little Ash curse."

His lips pinched. "Doesn't make it right. And before you think I had it easy, Nicola wasn't exactly a warm parental figure. She cared for me but in a tough-love kind of way."

"You obviously don't hate her for it, though. You keep in contact."

He rolled his big shoulders before tugging on his shirt. "She did her best, which is commendable given she lost her humanity early on in the Grimm Effect."

I pulled on the robe I'd worn to get to the pool before murmuring, "I still can't believe you came for me."

"Of course, I did. She had no right to take you."

"You risked yourself. Nicola told me of the route to get in and out of her home."

"Bah, I wasn't in any danger. I ran her security gauntlet all the time growing up."

"Fine, but you ditched your duties to the prince to

waste time fetching me." I grew tired of him making light of what I saw as a grand gesture.

"It was not a waste of time!" he practically bellowed. "You could have been hurt or killed by her actions."

"So you admit you did it because you worried about me." I couldn't have said why I needed that confirmation.

A mighty scowl twisted his face. "Yes, I worried. Happy?"

"Yes." I approached him so I could put my hands on his tense forearms. "Thank you. Thank you for rescuing me."

His expression melted. "I would do anything for you, princess."

I cupped his cheek. "My sweet Knight."

"Sweet?" he snorted. "Are you trying to ruin my reputation?"

My lips curved. "So sorry. I promise to not tell anyone."

"You'd better not," he grumbled, sweeping me into his arms.

"What are you doing?"

"Taking you back to the room."

"I can walk, you know."

"Don't care."

He really didn't. He carried me to the room,

ignoring those who called out to him on the way, and then, despite our pinging phones, made fierce love to me that ended with him whispering, "Maybe I should have let you make the bargain with my mother."

It killed me to realize he feared I'd break his heart.

17

The rest of that day and the next, Levi didn't let me out of his sight. If he went to check on the prince, I went too. When I had to talk to the ball organizer about the stage setup, he sat in, arms crossed, glowering in a corner. On the outside, he seemed grumpier than usual, but that changed the moment we were alone.

Every few hours we'd head to our room, and the moment that door closed he'd kiss me. Touch me. Make my toes curl with pleasure. But there was a franticness to the lovemaking, as if he feared every time would be our last.

His dread proved contagious. It didn't help that the crush of Cinderellas outside had grown yet again, to the point actual guests cancelled. I couldn't blame them. No one wanted to be there when the prince had to face and ultimately disappoint them.

I didn't want to go to the ball either. The fact that I kept being taunted by nursery rhymes didn't help. I'd seen the banjo-playing cat again, singing the same song and, for some reason, kept finding wedding dress brochures every time I turned around.

What did it all mean?

Things came to a head late in the afternoon of the ball. Everyone walked around on eggshells, partially because Levi kept snapping but also because we kept having random Cinderellas somehow making it past security. The times they managed to make it into Killian's presence, we averted disaster by playing the part of a happily engaged couple, which sent them fleeing, oftentimes mumbling about how they didn't know what came over them.

Seeing as how it kept working, at least on an individual basis, I shouldn't have been surprised when, during our last planning session, Hannah brought up her idea again.

"You know, we might be able to avert catastrophe if Killian and Cinder make a public announcement."

The suggestion fell into a dead silence, broken by Levi's firm, "No."

Hannah glanced at her boss. "We have to do something. Many of those women outside are determined to snag the prince, by any means necessary. And before you even say it, no, we can't mow them down to solve the problem."

Better her saying it than me. I did worry about Levi's state of mind. This situation wouldn't be solved with violence even if it might devolve into it.

"Your ill-advised idea will paint a target on Cinder, or do you think they'll all just go 'Okay, the prince is engaged. Let's just leave,'" Levi offered, his tone mocking.

"It's been working so far," Hannah insisted.

"It has, but you forget that's been one-on-one," Levi pointed out. "This ball will have hundreds of potentials. Hundreds of threats. The moment Killian declares Cinder as his intended, chaos will break loose."

"Chaos is already here," Killian muttered.

Levi wasn't done though. "Ever stop to think that this plan might play into the curse's hands? After all, you've got a prince, and a true Cinderella, pledging themselves in front of hundreds. We can't predict what the magic will do to manipulate it so they get married for real."

"I would never go that far," I interjected, which swung his gaze my way.

"You agree with this plan?"

I shrugged. "It's not ideal, However, Hannah is

right. As it currently stands, my mere presence appears to be triggering. There's going to be trouble no matter what. And it's not just me who's got to be careful. Killian's going to keep having to deal with this, not to mention all those poor women, caught in the grips of the curse, thinking they have to marry the prince. It must be horrible to not be in charge of their own thoughts and emotions."

Levi's brow rose. "So you admit they're being controlled."

"Well, yes. I'd say that's obvious."

"And what makes you think you're stronger than the magic? If you pretend on such a large scale, who's to say the magic won't sweep in and make you truly believe Killian is your one true love?"

I opened my mouth to deny that would ever happen, only to remain quiet, because he raised a valid point. Could I prevail against the Grimm Effect if it truly concentrated on me? At the same time, could I really not do anything at all?

Torn, I didn't reply, so I was surprised when Levi offered a gruff, "Sorry. I don't mean to shit on the idea. I just want to be sure you've thought through the possible ramifications."

If we'd been alone, I might have said something about my love for him being stronger than any curse, but at the same time, that might be wishful thinking.

Plenty of happily married couples had been split by the Grimm Effect.

"Levi is right." Killian stood. "The temptation of us playing along might be more than any of us could resist."

"So what's the plan?" Hannah asked. "What are we supposed to do if all those Cinderellas start throwing their shoes at you?"

Killian offered a lopsided smile. "Duck? I used to be quite good at dodgeball."

With that, the meeting broke up as we went to our rooms to dress.

Levi remained quiet even when the door closed.

I put a hand on his arm. "Are you okay?"

"No," he sighed. "Why do I get this awful feeling everything changes after today?"

"Because it will. Once the ball is over, Killian will leave, and we'll move on to our next job for the bureau."

He glanced at me. "I wish that I believed that."

"You're really worried about the curse."

"Aren't you?"

"I told you before I'll only marry for love."

"But what if the Grimm Effect makes you believe you love the prince?"

I didn't make light of his concern. He was being honest with me. Sharing his fear.

I clasped his hand. "There is no curse in this world that will make me forget I love you."

He blinked.

I blushed because, oops, I'd done it. I said what had been in my heart since that realization in the Nixie's cave.

"You love me?" Said softly, with a stunned expression.

I nodded. "Very much."

The smile he bestowed almost melted me. "I love you, too, princess."

"So you see, you have nothing to worry about." I cupped his cheek. "There is no magic in this world that could change what's in my heart."

Poof.

Godmother's sudden appearance startled us both, especially since we'd been about to kiss.

"Children, we don't have time for hanky-panky. It's time to prepare for the ball." Godmother waved her wand in excitement.

"The mice already have my things ready." Indeed, my dress of pale pink hung on the curtain rod. My shoes, sensible ballerina flats, sat below it. I'd opted to not wear a flamboyant gown with a wide skirt because I didn't want to be the belle of the ball.

"Oh that won't do at all," muttered Godmother. "Much too plain."

Before I could protest, she waved her wand and my simple attire turned into a thing of intricate beauty. Still pale pink, but with silver threading creating a fine filigree atop it. The shoes turned silver and glittery. A tiara sat on the table beside Izzy, along with a necklace and earrings with matching diamonds.

"That's much too elaborate," I protested.

"Nonsense. Let's see how it looks on you."

Again, I could do nothing, as my clothes suddenly got replaced by the fancy gown that fit perfectly. My hair went from hanging around my shoulders to pinned atop my head, with the tiara perched atop. My nails gleamed with a lovely French pedicure. My face wore a subtle layer of makeup. A glance in the mirror showed the princess Levi claimed me to be.

"Wow." Levi whistled. "You are stunning."

The mice agreed and cheered.

I scowled. "I'm going to draw way too much attention."

"As you should. Tonight is special." Godmother clasped her hands.

"I just want it to be over with." I already couldn't wait to strip out of the finery and slip into bed with my lover.

"It's not too late to back out. Say the word and I will whisk you away," Levi offered.

I sighed. "I want to, more than you know, but I can't abandon Killian."

"Speaking of whom, we should probably head down in case he's getting cold feet," Levi drawled.

"Not so quick, Sir Knight. As her companion, you, too, need something a little more than your usual attire."

Levi barely had time to say, "Like fuck." His protest did not stop the magic from changing his clothes. He ended up in a black uniform, form-fitting with silver highlights, topped with shiny black boots. His hair received a magical trim, his five o'clock shadow shaved, and rather than a tiara, he wore a ring.

A ring that made him frown. "Where did you find this?" he asked Godmother. "I thought I lost this years ago diving in a wreck."

"The Nixie gave it to me when she popped in this afternoon for a visit via my goldfish pond. She thought you might have a use for it." Godmother beamed. "Don't you both look marvelous. Now off I must go. You're not the only people who need my attention tonight. So many Cinderellas looking for a miracle."

Off she poofed, almost maniacal in her excitement. So much for Godmother wanting to break the fairytale curse. It appeared instead she'd been swept into the story full steam.

"You look very handsome," I stated as Levi frowned and fidgeted.

"It's too fancy."

"Well, it is a ball."

He grimaced. "I'm a warrior, not a prince."

"Suck it up, buttercup," I quipped, using an expression I'd heard Blanche say more than once.

His jaw dropped.

My lips curved. "In a few hours, this ball will be over, and I can't wait to strip you out of it."

"Here's to hoping nothing goes sideways." At least he'd not lost his sense of doom and gloom.

"Shall we?" I asked, placing my hand on his bicep.

"After you, princess."

He didn't say much as we headed down to the ballroom. Even this deep in the hotel, we could hear the potential Cinderellas getting rowdy outside as the time for the ball neared.

Killian awaited on the dais erected at the far end of the room, looking every inch the prince with his white uniform trimmed in gold braid. It shouldn't have surprised to see some of the bureau agents in attendance. Hood and her wolf, Aidan, dressed in red and black. Hilda in a gown of sequined green. But I gasped at the sight of Belle decked in a gown of shimmering gold, her hair crowned in roses.

When I greeted Belle and stated, "You're looking prettier than a princess," she grimaced.

"Some old woman showed up and changed my outfit, and I don't have time to run home to change." It had to be Godmother. How odd.

Hannah and Gerome wore matching black uniforms of the non-magical variety, same as the other Knights roaming the outskirts of the room. More than I'd actually met.

At my glance, Levi murmured, "We called in reinforcements."

Good idea.

Levi walked me to the dais, where Killian fidgeted.

"Is it too late to cancel?" he murmured.

"I'm surprised you agreed to this ball in the first place if you hate the idea so much."

"Did I not mention this was my mother's idea?" Killian sighed. "Sometimes I think it would be easier to just get married. At least it would get her off my back."

"Maybe you'll meet the right person tonight!" I chirped.

"Maybe..." Killian muttered, looking to his left where Belle had her face buried in a book. Only she would think to bring a novel to a party.

Levi sidled close to murmur, "It's almost time. I won't be far if you need me." He squeezed my hand before striding off and didn't notice his ring falling from his hand. I scooped it, but before I could return it to him, Hannah bellowed, "Heads up! The Cinderellas broke through the security line and are coming."

I could hear them. Like a stampede of wild beasts in heels and taffeta, they came charging for the ballroom, sweeping in and heading for the dais, pausing before it to stare dreamily at Killian. A few hundred hopeful faces of all ages and backgrounds.

To Killian's credit, he didn't run away.

I, on the other hand, really wished I'd chosen to follow Levi, as my spot on the stage made me a focus of attention. AKA glares. I could handle being stared at, but the mutters worried me.

"Look at that slut, thinking she's better than us."

"I'm way hotter than her."

"She wouldn't be so pretty with a broken nose."

But the comment that chilled me most? *"If she's dead, the prince can't choose her."*

I wanted to run for Levi, my shield in the coming storm. A storm we should have avoided. The moment the first Ash potential appeared, we should have cancelled the ball regardless of Killian's mother's wishes. Who ever thought going through with this was a good idea?

The Grimm Effect of course. It must have manipulated us to get us here. It wanted something to happen. How else to explain the chaos spreading in the room?

It didn't help that the Cinderellas fed on each other's urgency.

At least they quieted when Killian grabbed the microphone to say, "Good evening, ladies."

A cacophony of screams erupted, and a few women fainted.

"I love you!" hollered someone in bright purple.

"Screw her, I'm your true love," yelled another.

"Pick me!"

Killian shifted, uncomfortable and hesitating. I neared him and murmured, "You've got this. Just a few hours and it will be over."

Killian nodded and took a deep breath. "Thank you for coming. I am pleased to announce that my meeting—"

"Get to the point!" A woman in royal blue from head to toe, which included heavy eyeshadow, interrupted from the front. "You need to choose your bride."

"I'm afraid that won't be happening." Killian tried to be honest, and the wave of boos just about knocked us over.

I glanced at Levi and saw him murmuring with Hannah, who then sidled to my side as Killian tried to explain that, while he appreciated the effort they'd made, he wasn't here to get married.

Not what the crowd wanted to hear, and they

began pushing for the dais, ignoring the ring of Knights that formed a wall to hold them back.

Hannah murmured in my ear, "I think it's time for plan B." Plan B being a fake engagement.

"But Levi—"

"Says do what you have to. This is going to get ugly otherwise."

I glanced at Levi, and he met my gaze, blank and stoic, but he did give me a slight nod.

With that permission, I moved to Killian's side. He held the microphone with a deer-in-headlights expression.

I whispered in his ear, "Time to get engaged."

He gave me a startled look before his eyes cleared with understanding. His shoulders went back, and he spoke once more. "I'm sorry, ladies. I must say that you look resplendent. Absolutely ravishing, however, my heart has already been captured." He grabbed my hand and held it aloft. "I've found my Cinderella, and she's agreed to be my wife."

18

At Killian's announcement, dead silence fell.

I waited for that switch to turn off and turn the potentials back into themselves.

A few visibly shook themselves and began pushing their way to the exit. But too many, far too many, remained, and the loud one in front chose to escalate things.

"If that's true, then marry her. Right here. Right now," Royal Blue demanded.

My jaw dropped. Married? That had never been part of the plan.

Luckily, Killian had a smooth reply. "Such a special occasion deserves proper planning."

"You can always have a second ceremony later,"

Royal Blue insisted. "If she's your true love, then you'll marry her right now."

I glanced at Levi, who frowned.

Killian attempted to defuse with another excuse. "I'm afraid that's impossible. We have no one to officiate."

"I can perform the ceremony." The same woman with her satin blue gown stepped forward, her chin tilted stubbornly. "I'm an ordained minister. I can hear your vows."

"But my mother—"

"Can watch the replay," snarled the woman offering her services. "Because I don't believe you. I think you're lying because you don't think we're good enough for you." Her claim brought an ugly murmur from those standing at her back.

"Nonsense, you're all lovely. But to get married here and now? That would be—"

"Romantic," someone shouted, to which many added their agreement.

"Or are you lying?" challenged the woman in the front row. "It ain't nice to lie."

I'm sure all the Knights noticed as some shoes came off and got held in one hand, ready to be fired.

I half expected Levi to hustle me off the stage, but a quick peek showed him standing still as a statue.

Hannah muttered, "Just do it. We can have it annulled later."

True. It wouldn't be a real marriage, just something to appease the rabid crowd of wannabe princesses. Still, it didn't feel right.

Didn't feel right to stand facing Killian, while the woman began reciting, "Dearly beloved…"

I glanced at Levi, standing rigid, stony-faced. Holding in his emotions. Not speaking up because he didn't want to escalate the situation, even if it killed him inside. Marrying Killian, even if a sham, would hurt him. Hurt the person I loved most. Yet if I didn't, the mob of potentials might tear me limb from limb.

His pain or mine, which mattered more?

I took a step back from the prince and shook my head. "I'm sorry. I can't do this. It's not right."

At my words, once more, silence fell.

Killian cocked his head and murmured, "I understand."

He did, but I wanted Levi to realize what I did and why.

I walked across the dais to him. Levi bristled with confusion. "What are you doing?" he murmured.

"The right thing," I said. "I told you before I will only marry for love, and since you're the man who holds my heart…"

"Princess." He hissed my name as I grabbed his hand.

"You lost something." I slid the ring he'd dropped onto his finger, a perfect fit that should have never fallen in the first place. I looked him in the eye before asking loudly and proudly, "Will you marry me?"

Levi's cheeks turned a ruddy color, and I heard Gerome snicker, but to my pleasure—and relief—Levi nodded. "It would be my greatest honor to marry you."

A chorus of "Aahs," followed, and I beamed at my fiancé.

I'd done it. My love had made me brave enough to do the unthinkable.

"Guess we're starting over," complained Royal Blue, the volunteer minister.

"Er, what?" I whirled to ask with confusion.

"If you love him, then you shouldn't have a problem marrying him right now," Royal Blue taunted.

"But Levi's mother isn't here," I protested.

"Nicola hates gatherings," Levi murmured as he led me across the stage to stand in front of the self-appointed minister.

"Are you sure?" I asked him.

"More than anything in this world," he replied.

Royal Blue, looking smug, cleared her throat and

said, "Dearly beloved, we are gathered here today in search of our prince but now bear witness to one of our Ash sisters finding love…"

Royal Blue spoke, and yet I barely heard a word as I stared into Levi's eyes. A man I'd fallen head over heels for.

He held my gaze, steady and handsome, even slightly smiling because of me. I hoped to keep him smiling for the rest of our lives.

"And you may now kiss your bride." The ceremony finished.

As my lips pressed to Levi's—now my lawfully wedded husband—the mood in the room shifted, and once more, the tension became palpable. The brief moment of peace when I'd rejected Killian in favor of Levi dissipated, making the prince once more the main focus.

"Uh-oh," Killian muttered as hundreds of wannabe brides eyed him with unnatural hunger.

Even worse, they surged for the dais, the few that grappled with the Knights leaving openings for others to try and rush the stage. It led my new husband tucking me behind his back and drawing his gun.

"You can't shoot them," I pleaded.

"I will if they try to hurt you," he promised. I couldn't fault him for wanting to protect me.

The Knights and agents retreated to form a ring

between us and the curse-maddened women. Levi left my side and joined them, a wall between us and the violence trying to erupt as women held their shoes aloft, screaming, "Pick me!"

All might have been lost if not for the sudden and shrill scream of the woman in emerald green taffeta peeking between Gerome's legs. "No! What are you doing? You can't pick her."

Wait, pick who? What happened?

The chaos subsided, and a sudden silence fell as all eyes suddenly went to Prince Killian, who knelt in front of Belle as he picked up the book she'd dropped. He handed it to her with a murmured, "I think this is yours."

"Thank you, dear prince." Belle offered a beaming smile and only because I knew her did I recognize the fakeness of it.

"It is I who must thank you." Killian rose and clasped Belle's hands. "It would appear I was mistaken in my affection, confused because of how often you were in close proximity, but you, and only you, dear and fair Belle, are my one true love."

"Oh, Killian." Belle batted her lashes so fast they almost took off.

Levi retreated to my side to murmur, "What's happening?"

I whispered back, "She's saving the prince."

Killian whipped out a ring box and popped it open. He held it out so that the diamond within glinted. "Please tell me you'll marry me and make me the happiest prince alive."

I saw Belle struggle to not roll her eyes as she held out her hand and crooned, "It would be my pleasure, oh sweet prince."

A moan of disappointment arose as the ring went on her finger. Dozens began to turn and leave, only to pause as someone shouted, "If she's really your Cinderella, then marry her, now!"

Belle's eyes widened, and Killian stiffened before he tried once more to delay. "We can't have two marriages in one day."

Not according to the crowd.

"Marry him. Marry him." The chant grew in volume as the women who'd been jilted insisted on him going through with the farce.

Levi uttered a soft warning to the Knights and agents. "Everyone get ready to evacuate the prince on my count."

Once more, Belle rose to the occasion. She lifted her head and shouted, "Very well. You want to see me marry the prince, then so be it. If the lady who married Cinder and her Knight would do us the honor?"

For the second time that night, Royal Blue conducted a ceremony this time featuring a shell-shocked prince and a stony-faced bureau agent. I commended Belle for taking the drastic step, even as I mentally made notes on what I'd have to do to get it annulled.

When it ended with "You may kiss the bride," their lips touched, and was it me, or did I see a spark?

Whatever the case, a visible tremor went through the room as the curse suddenly lifted from all those women. Some of them began to sob. Others stomped angrily away. Angry because they'd not gotten the prince or because the Grimm Effect had duped them?

Didn't matter. In moments, the ballroom emptied of Cinderellas.

The ball was over.

19

To say we stood there slightly shell-shocked would be putting it mildly. Two marriages and not a single death. The evening had definitely not gone as expected.

At least in my case, I came out a winner. Levi was my husband. But Killian and Belle...

I glanced over and saw Prince Killian rake fingers through his hair and Belle looking bemused.

I hustled to her side to exclaim, "Fast thinking marrying the prince! And don't you worry, I'll have it annulled ASAP."

To my surprise, Killian shook his head. "Don't be too quick." He glanced at Belle. "If you don't mind, I could use a bit of a respite from having shoes tossed at me."

"Pity the story wasn't about panties. They'd hurt less," Belle quipped, and my mouth rounded in shock.

However, the prince chuckled in amusement. "These past few days have been insane. When did the curse get so bad?"

"Recently," my flat reply. "We've noticed not only an increase in reenactments but a darker edge to many. It's as if something is agitating the Grimm Effect and it's taken an ominous turn."

"There has to be something we can do," Killian stated. "And before you say it, I know people have been looking—"

Belle interrupted. "Not really. Most who dared to try and investigate the root of the curse found themselves roped into some of the uglier stories. The kind that don't end well. Needless to say, it's led to a lack of curiosity, as most people don't have a death wish."

"Maybe what happened tonight will put both your stories to bed." I offered them a branch of hope.

"Maybe..." Belle sounded skeptical, whereas Killian offered a hesitant, "Do you think so? I'd like to believe it's over, but I do worry an annulment will bring back the madness."

Once more, Belle glanced at Killian. "You know, we could use this break from the curse to work on cancelling it permanently."

"I thought you said people tried and got punished for it," Killian reminded.

"None of them have been as determined as me, though," Belle remarked, and I, for one, could vouch for her tenacious nature.

"Where would we even start?" Killian asked.

Having seen Belle's research room, I wasn't surprised she had a quick reply. "In the town that first reported the Grimm Effect. There has to be a reason it began there and spread. I say we start our search in that area."

"We?" Killian sounded surprised, and yet he quickly nodded. "Yes, let's do it."

"Not alone." Levi showed he'd been listening despite huddling with his Knights. "Hannah and Gerome will accompany you."

"We will?" Hannah didn't hide her surprise.

"Yes," Levi stated with a tone that brooked no argument. "You are hereby assigned to the prince and his bride until further notice."

"Aye, aye, boss." Hannah rolled her eyes as she saluted him. As for Gerome, he grunted.

As we dispersed, I half expected Levi to whisk me away. After all, it was our wedding night, but my new husband had business to attend to. Not willingly, but I wouldn't let him shirk his duty. Despite the Ash potentials dispersing, we couldn't be complacent because I had a feeling the curse wasn't done with us yet.

While Levi dished out orders to the Knights, I prepared for the coming evening with Rory as my bodyguard in the hall outside the open door. The dress stayed on, but I took down my hair from its intricate coiffe. The mice brushed it out until it crackled but fled out of sight when Levi arrived. Izzy hustled to a spot under the dresser. Guess they knew what would be coming next. Anticipation curled my toes.

My new husband entered and firmly shut the door. His expression smoldered, and my mouth went dry. Odd because we'd been intimate, so why did it feel different this time?

"Hello, husband," I said softly.

"Wife," he stated with a low rumble. "*My* wife."

I shivered at the possessiveness of it. This was the man I would spend my life with. My partner. My lover. My Knight in shining armor.

I couldn't have said who moved first, only that we came together for a passionate kiss that had him lifting me from the floor and twirling me around.

When he set me on my feet, I laughed, a little breathless.

"What's so funny?"

"The way things worked out. Guess Godmother knew you and I were in love."

"What makes you say that?"

"Why else give you a ring? A ring that fits snugly on your finger and yet happened to fall in front of me. A ring that served as my shoe. She knew I wouldn't marry Killian."

"I'll admit I was a tad a worried," Levi admitted.

"I'd have let those Ash potentials tear me apart before I hurt you," I admitted.

"Yeah, that wouldn't have happened. I have good aim." A dark reply and yet I saw it for what he meant. He loved me too much to let me come to harm.

"I love you," I murmured.

"I love you more than anything, my beautiful princess wife."

"Then kiss me and make this a night to remember," I demanded, and he strove to make my wish come true.

His mouth found mine for hungry kiss, which lasted only a moment before he nipped my bottom lip and growled, "Let's get you out of that dress."

Mmm... I wouldn't mind getting him naked, too. The uniform looked good on him, but stripped of it with all his flesh and muscles for me to admire was even better.

Levi made quick work of the buttons on the back of my dress, and once released, the whole thing slid down my body to the floor and he groaned. "I will never tire of seeing your gorgeous body."

"How about instead of looking, you touch?" I teased.

Levi dragged me close, but rather than resume our kiss, his lips went to my neck, where he nibbled and nipped before traveling down to my breasts. He cupped them, squeezed them together, and smothered his face in the crevice he formed. When he sucked my taut nipples, I gasped and held on to his head, tugging at his hair while mashing him against my breasts, telling him without words what I wanted.

He sucked them. His tongue swirling around the tips. His teeth pinching my flesh, making me gasp.

My knees buckled at all the sensations, but Levi was there to catch me. Holding me firmly, he walked us to the bed. The backs of my legs hit it first, and I sat down, parting my thighs for him to slip between. His cock jutted proudly from his groin, and I grabbed it for a tug, which led to him sucking in a breath.

"My naughty princess," he breathed.

"About to get naughtier," I teased, switching my position so I could bring my mouth level with his shaft.

With one hand gripping him firmly, I latched onto the head of him, and his cock twitched. He groaned when I pulled him into my mouth, suctioning the length of him while sliding his shaft in and out. I found a rhythm and bobbed my head along his length, excited by the way he hummed in pleasure, loving the tug as his fingers threaded my hair.

I could feel him getting harder. Thicker. Pulsing. And I wanted it. Wanted him to come in my mouth, but he had other plans.

"My turn," he growled.

I wasn't about to argue. I lay on the bed, legs parted, wet and quivering as he lay between my thighs and buried his face. His tongue lapped at me, long, slow strokes that went across my clit and slid between my nether lips.

"Oh." Pretty sure he didn't need to hear my moans to know how much I enjoyed his mouth on me. My pleasure built quickly. Coiling tight within, making my channel clench, which led me to whisper, "I need you inside me."

I wanted to climax around him. To feel him inside me as I came.

Instead, his tongue went to my clit and his fingers found the moist core of me, penetrating, stroking, pushing me over the edge.

I cried out as I orgasmed, a sweet ripple that had him grunting before he covered my body with his. The tip of his throbbing cock poked at my sex, wetting the head before he began pushing it in. The width of him stretched me, and the length of him reached my sweet spot inside. He thrust, deep, firm plunges into my still-quivering sex. Over and over. He stroked my dying orgasm into a new coiling pressure. I tightened around his pulsing cock. Encouraged him with the dig of my nails in his back.

And when I came a second time, he joined me, bellowing my name. "I love you, Cinder."

"Oh, how I love you, too, my sweet Knight," I purred as I came down from that blissful high.

"How did I get so lucky?" he murmured, cradling me close as the aftershocks tingled between my legs.

"It wasn't luck but fate," I declared.

He snorted. "A fate that kept conspiring to keep us apart."

I had to wonder because, after all, all those things that happened only drew us closer together.

We made love a second time, slower, more sensually, and finished with our gazes locked. So intimate.

But also sticky. "I need to bathe," I declared when he tucked me into him, readying to sleep.

"As my princess desires." Levi rolled out of bed and headed to the bathroom to run the bath. When I entered, I noticed he'd even added bubbles, but before I could step into the steaming pleasure, a head rose from the tub.

Nicola emerged, her green hair crowned in suds.

Upon seeing her, I worried that Levi might be wrong about the wedding. Would she be angry we'd gotten married without her?

"Mother, what have I said about visiting me in the bathroom?" Levi stated in a chiding tone, his bulky nude body providing a shield for mine.

"I won't be here long. Just wanted to say congratulations. You've chosen a fine bride, even if her hips are too narrow, but with today's medical advancements, the babe in her belly should be born without issue."

I blinked. Pretty sure Levi stopped breathing.

Nicola smirked. "I'll leave you two to enjoy your wedding night. But will add, don't forget your promise."

With that, she sank under the water in the tub, while I rocked on my heels trying to wrap my head around the fact I was pregnant.

Levi faintly said, "Did she just imply..."

I nodded and grabbed his hand to place it on my belly. "We're going to be parents."

Levi keeled over and splashed into the tub, only barely missing smacking his head. I panicked and ran for aid since I couldn't lift him out.

"Gerome! Help. Levi fainted."

"Like fuck," his initial reply.

"I told him I was pregnant."

At those words, Gerome came at a run to help, and

for the first time ever, I heard the quiet man laugh before he grunted, "Boss man is gonna make a great dad."

And a great husband, because this was my story and I would live a happily ever after.

Epilogue

A FEW WEEKS LATER...

"Princess, I'm home," Levi bellowed, walking through the door to our new place. An actual house with lots of bedrooms because I doubted we'd stop at one baby. All that extra space meant my friends were in their glory. The mice had been burrowing into the walls to create themselves cozy homes. Charlotte loved the dusty attic that came with built-in friends. As for Izzy, he adored the garden out back and spent much time sunbathing on the lip of the fountain, a fountain that spewed Nicola when the mood to visit struck her.

It drove Levi nuts that she kept popping in, but I didn't mind. After all, the Nixie wanted to be a part of her grandchild's life. But even better, she became the mother I never had.

Levi found me in the home office where I'd begun

working almost every other day, skipping the ones when the morning sickness hit me hard.

"Hi," I chirped, seeing him. "Give me a second to finish up this email."

"No problems?" he asked, sitting on the corner of my desk.

"Nope." As a matter of fact, the nursery rhymes involving me stopped the moment we got married. No more singing cats or fish in the tub. Although it took more than a week of Levi hovering before I could convince him I didn't need watching twenty-four-seven.

"I brought you a present," he stated.

"Ooh." I couldn't help but clap in excitement. I'd never gotten gifts growing up.

"Give me a second." He left and returned carrying a box with holes.

Even before he pulled off the lid, I knew what to expect.

I still burst into tears as I snagged the little brown cub and hugged him close.

"This little guy was going to be shipped off to a zoo," Levi explained. "Mama and papa bear had a run-in with a gun-toting Goldilocks."

"He's perfect," I exclaimed, rubbing my nose against the cub's.

"Thought he'd make you happy." Levi looked

smug.

"You make me happy," my sappy reply.

He did. Where I'd once complained about Levi being a trial to deal with, I now saw how we complemented each other. I could only hope Belle would find the same happy ending to her story.

The day after the mock wedding, aboard Prince Killian's private jet.

Belle smirked as she flopped into a ridiculously comfortable chair. "Now this is what I call traveling in style."

"Perfect for our honeymoon," Killian declared. "Although you'll have to forgive me. I forgot to pack my lingerie."

Her lips curved. The man did have a better sense of humor than she'd have expected from a royal. "I think you'd look dashing in a black lace teddy."

At the back of the plane, Hannah coughed. She and Gerome would be accompanying Belle and Killian as they sought the origin of the Grimm Effect. It still surprised Belle that the prince agreed to come. After all, he'd technically just beaten his curse. Yet, when she'd told him about her idea to investigate the possible origin of the curse, he'd been gung ho.

Killian laughed. He did that often. "I'll keep that in mind. Anything I can get you?"

"A prince serving a commoner?"

"A prince should always service his princess."

And he meant it. She didn't have to lift a finger. If her water got low, he replenished. He made sure the snack tray remained full, all the while providing witty banter.

Belle simply reclined and sighed. "This is the life."

"Have you ever been married?" he asked out of the blue.

"Nope. Can't. The curse isn't happy I jilted the beast, and since then, any attempts at being amorous are met with a new beast."

"Hold on. Are you saying you don't even date?"

"Not anymore because a single kiss and, bam, suddenly I end up with a hairy jerk who wants to do the horizontal, bestial tango."

"Yikes," he replied, only to add, "We kissed, and I'm still me."

She'd thought about it and came to a single conclusion. "Probably because you're the prince of another story."

"And the curse doesn't like to double up." He

nodded. "This town we're visiting... Anything I should know about it?"

"It's not real interesting, other than the fact the first confirmed Grimm Effect case started there, although that wasn't known for a decade due to poor record-keeping in the beginning. One Deborah Goodwin woke up and ghsindopliink—" Belle's words suddenly emerged garbled as her mouth twisted violently and her jaw cracked. All of her torqued something odd.

And it hurt. Like really hurt! Not that she could scream. She went rigid and momentarily blind.

When the pain subsided, and she spoke, her voice emerged huskier than usual. "That was weird."

"Um, Belle..."

"What?" she asked, eyeing him and wondering at his shocked mien.

"How to say this?" Rather than tell her, Killian held up his phone, and she wondered why until she spotted the monster reflected on the screen.

Wait, not just any monster.

The beast she could see with the furry face and mane?

That's me.

. . .

Cinder's Trial

IT WOULD APPEAR Belle has been caught up in a twisted version of her story. That's the bad news. In good news, she's about to embark on an adventure to put a stop to the Grimm Effect once and for all. Get ready for Belle's Quest.

www.ingramcontent.com/pod-product-compliance
Lightning Source LLC
LaVergne TN
LVHW031540060526
838200LV00056B/4579